Rita Singh

Magical Moon

FIRST EDITION

Afternoon Stories Press

First printing June 2019   ISBN: 978-1-7344465-9-3

MY PAGES, each a blank note
Were leaves on a tree
Until evening's pen wrote
Spells on me

The ink of the dusk
Wasn't yet dry
When the wind, too brusque
Came striding by

The ink, seeking shelter
Streaked to one side
Helter and skelter
Words sought to hide

So each story they spin
Is a streaked, jumbled spell
What enchantment lies within
No one can tell

–Ledger entry 5-4-3-2

Let the magic begin each time with these words: Lorem ipsum dolor sit amet, consectetur adipiscing elit. Aenean auctor neque at semper pulvinar. Phasellus mollis dolor eu est gravida, a tristique quam tincidunt. Quisque vulputate elit id accumsan ullamcorper. Donec porta interdum est hendrerit tristique. Sed dictum egestas dolor, non tempor eros ornare sed. Nulla sagittis lacinia massa, vel venenatis libero luctus in. In hac habitasse platea dictumst. Vivamus eget arcu velit. Nunc maximus justo sed purus ultricies tincidunt. Sed accumsan, nisl non porttitor placerat, metus risus eleifend augue, tincidunt euismod nisi quam quis mauris. Aenean vel iaculis orci. Nulla euismod magna vitae est ultrices auctor. Donec rutrum pulvinar nisl a consectetur...

Preface

This book is set in the land of the magical moon, which works in whimsical ways, but has many parallels to our real world.

On the night of the harvest moon, if you happen to have the magic book of runes, you can evoke its magic, which then takes you on spellbinding adventures into the land of the magical moon. The book of runes has answers to all the questions in the world, which must be phrased and written in a certain way for the spell to be evoked. Once a question is successfully asked, someone appears to read the answers to you – because the answers are in runes, in a language you can't read. The people who are sent to read each answer live and work in the land of the magical moon.

The poems in this book recount the adventures that follow in the wake of thirteen questions, with the thirteen characters who are sent by the magical moon to read the answers. The collection of whimsical characters in this book includes Aflatoon, a genial genie who is generally confused, an angel, and agricultural scholar, a politician who can't be clear about an answer even when it is clearly written for him to read, and many others. The land of the magical moon is never described as such – every adventure adds a few clues, some threads to a beautiful tapestry that begins to emerge as the book progresses.

Through these magical adventures, this book also addresses serious questions about life and this world. Questions that are so down to earth that some appear jarring or embarassing. Nonetheless, they are asked by millions of children around the world in different forms, and often their answers are difficult to provide.

This book was written in stolen time. When I wrote these adventures, often at nights when I would have a few physically restful moments after a difficult and exhausting day, I would look through my window at the magical moon, and dream about a world where moments of leisure would be plentiful. I have yet to find that world. When I finished this book, I began to write a sequel to it. However, I couldn't finish it. Like all things in life, it abruptly stopped. That incomplete sequel – with the one adventure that I wrote in it – is provided as-is at the end of this book. Perhaps some day I will finish it, sitting in my attic in the land of the magical moon.

Contents

Magical Moon

QUI DOLOREM ipsum, quia dolor
I scratched that out, and wrote some more
In my attic on that night in June
I'd found the runes for a magical moon

Not the moon that made white wolves cry
But the kind that answered questions why
A tree was burned while another grew
The seasons turned, or eagles flew

I had to write, if I had to know
Along these lines that quivered so
Each letter that I wrote awry
Had to stay on them, you'd wonder why

I wrote on a parchment I had found
Beside a book that was strangely bound
In something that looked quite baroque
And felt like wood and clay and smoke

I'd touched it and had known somehow
That I couldn't open it for now
I'd also known, on that magical night
What I had to do, what I had to write

The parchment that lay right beside
Had runes like leaves of autumn, dried
As I picked it up, they fell beneath
And the strangest lines lay underneath!

They were wicked wavered, swayed around
But your questions had to stand their ground
So here I stood, too amazed for fright
With a pen in hand on that moonlit night

If you finished right, then very soon
A breeze would hum a magical tune
It would puff on the magic book, a spell
Of a million sheets, though you couldn't tell

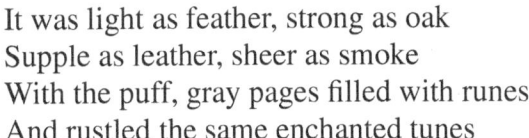

It was light as feather, strong as oak
Supple as leather, sheer as smoke
With the puff, gray pages filled with runes
And rustled the same enchanted tunes

Then the magical moon would send a ray
On the page that settled, smokey gray
The rays would light, in your spellbound sight
Some lines that would glow brightest white

The lines would hold in mystic cast
An answer to the question asked
Not in plain words like "Quia dolor"
But in runes from the times of yore

The runes would shimmer until when
A gust of wind would come again
The gust would usher magical things
Like a raven with a swallow's wings

Who'd then read out the lines to you
So you would know the answer too
And then the page would fade away
In a moment turn from white to gray

The stars outside would crowd around
The window as you'd look, spellbound
A million would then wink at you
And want to know what you now knew

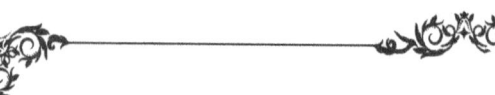
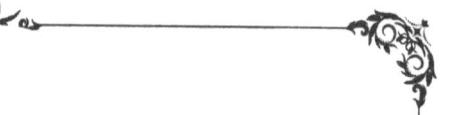

If you answered, they would then disperse
Into the night sky's universe
If you didn't, you'd forget it too
And never know what you now knew

You may wonder how I knew as much
That things would happen such and such
A spell blew over me that night
As I stood in the bright moonlight

On quivering lines I wrote some more
Qui dolorem ipsum, quia dolor
You may wonder why I chose such words
Just flecks and fragments, shreds and sherds

If I wrote full words, wrote them right
If they formed a question, then I might
Have an answer that I needn't know
And so I scrawled "...quia dolor"

In an hour or so of writing thus
I looked up when I heard a fuss
Some odd scuffling noises by the sill
Soft squeals and thuds and a tiny trill

Three pairs of eyes of the cutest coons
Looked in at me, like six bright moons
The smallest one with the tiny trill
Crept in, tip-pawed to me until

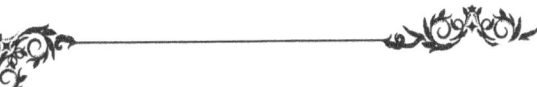

It was very close, looking up at me
And in the moonlight I could see
In its snout it held a glowing pen
A magical one, I saw right then

I somehow knew the magical moon
Had sent a friend to me: this coon
So I softly patted him, and then
Thanked him, and gently took the pen

When I held it on the lines, and tried
To stay on them with the writing side
It magically moved! And wrote for me!
"Qui dolorem ipsum, one two three"

In lovely swirls it wrote the words
With the grace of winds and soaring birds
It waltzed before my dazzled eyes
Like a dancer glides on glittering ice

I heard a sound and turned around
My friend I found, poking the ground
"Don't you – ever – steal a thing again!"
"That pen, I'm afraid, is a stolen pen!"

As the little coon rubbed his ear
Mom coon said sternly "Do you hear?"
"I'm *so* sorry," she said to me
"That pen must be returned, you see.."

6

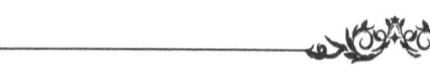

So I reached for it, but lo and behold
What do I see but scrolled in bold
Perfectly strung on a quivering line
Words that read: "Say that's fine"

"That's fine!" I said, "I understand"
"This pen must be from a magic land"
"We must find out, and so must we"
"Find an address and an addressee"

For a while it seemed the magic pen
Stood silent like a sage, and then
Swirled the words "Now hold me tight"
"Speak out your question, and I will write"

"It must be clear, must be well thought"
"It must not – ever – begin with *What*"
"It must not intrude, must not spy"
"Must not offend, must not have an *I*"

"It mustn't be greedy, must not be bad"
"It mustn't have horrors, not a tad"
"So ask away, don't be wary or shy"
"Questions may only begin with *Why*"

I gazed at the words, calligraphed so fine
Perfectly placed on a quivering line
Like a bird that rides a swinging wire
Like smoke that wraps a writhing fire

The Questions

I CLOSED my eyes, and all was still
Questions many began to mill
As they formed in a perfect row
Each one a star, would glint and glow

When I chose one, it moved aside
To a constellation on the side
I picked a few, some big some small
Just some – I couldn't ask them all!

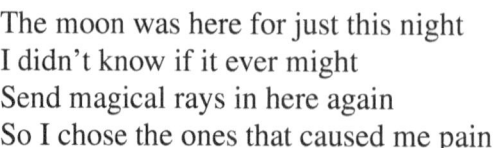

The moon was here for just this night
I didn't know if it ever might
Send magical rays in here again
So I chose the ones that caused me pain

The stars danced by, a hundred one
My list a dozen long when done
They waited for their answers there
Ablaze with beauty par compare

Then soon there rang a trill afar
The coon had caught the smallest star!
It brushed by me and placed in line
The thirteenth question just in time

Tommy

THE PEN was poised on the quivering lines
The leaves were rustling on the vines
The window curtains flapped along
The breeze whistled a soft low song

I asked the question right on top
From Mom coon's eye fell a large teardrop
The whistling breeze caught its breath
The rustling leaves stood still as death

My close friend Tommy lived next door
He was six, and his brother was four
He came to school with untied shoestrings
Wore rumpled clothes, brought broken things

This began just two summers ago
When his brother was two, he was four
My question now began with a "Why"
I hoped it was one that didn't pry

No one had told the brothers, I heard
Tommy told me they often wondered
If some wizard could tell them why
"Why did Tommy's mommy have to die?"

The breeze blew softly, pages stirred
The pen wrote quietly every word
The restless lines slowed down until
The last word written, they were still

On the pages, like dulcimer links
Runes harmonized in sparkling inks
Impacted by the breeze, these spells
Rang out like Corinthian bells

Like a tempest in a silent brook
Now the pages of that silent book
Flew open, rustled, crackled, fanned
As though controlled by a wizard's hand

With each note, searching south and north
Its pages ruffled, back and forth
Then a page fell open, smokey gray
And the moon streamed in a dazzling ray

On it, some lines glowed brightest white
With the answer that I sought tonight
As I tried hard to read the words
I heard cheeps, and chirps, and tweets of birds!

Startled, I turned to the window when
Little birds hopped in – two, five, ten
Then more and more and more of them
Until it there was intense mayhem!

On that starry night each little bird
Wore a tiny coat with hemline furred
Colored bright white, green, pink, or blue
Like hummingbirds of the richest hue

They arranged themselves in colored rows
Then one hopped on li'l coon's nose
The coon went up to the glowing page
And the bird it, grim as a sage

In a treble, soft and mellow tone
Read: "Though the soothing wind had blown"
"It would return with a treasure trove"
"Of more abundant, deeper love"

It seemed a fragment of some lore
Or a story from the times before
The bird flew back, and its refrain
Seemed solemnly to now explain

"The lives of all are like rain-song"
"Some short, some middling, and some long"
The somber tone of the bird now fell
"Sadly, Tommy's Mommy wasn't well"

"She lost to an illness she'd endure"
"For which no one had found a cure"
"But the answer lies in how wind blows"
"Flowing past, it both comes and goes"

"Her love is where the brothers go"
"In the sunshine, trees and plants that grow"
"She's always with them now, you know"
"She's left, but her love will never go"

"She's always very close to him"
"In the meadow and the babbling stream"
"On the road he walks, the wind that blows"
"No matter where little Tommy goes"

"He only has to look around"
"And love them back, all things around"
The birds now chorused from each row
"Yes, Tommy's Mommy loves him so!"

Birdsong swelled up, in crescendo
And then lowered, decrescendo
It paced in waves and andante
Until the music waned away

The best orchestra I had heard
With a bow, then the conductor bird
Amid applause, walked off the floor
And then returned for an encore

The magic book of runes grew thin
Its million pages faded in
Until it lay, silently where
Smokey gray, it was barely there

At the window now I saw a flare
Curious stars were crowded there
"The brothers ask us this each day"
"Tell us, so we know what to say!"

They listened nodding, quite solemn
They'd tell them when they wished on them
They waited, then were quietly gone
The little birds had also flown

There was no one there, very soon
As we gazed at the magical moon
The coon then poked me, eyes in crease
"Do ask the second question please!"

The Angel

THE SECOND question, strong as wool
Was about a dear friend at my school
While all came in, laughed and played
My friend was in hospice, where he stayed

The quivering lines were rather still
As I read the question out until
The pen finished its delicate scroll
Like a wreath of flowers, large and small

"Why is Jimmy ill, why won't he live?"
"Is it something someone won't forgive?"
The night was quiet, the moon was gray
The stars stopped twinkling in dismay

This had no answer, all were sure
For Jimmy's ailment had no cure
What if magic couldn't answer that?
The book of runes couldn't answer that?

If there was no answer to be found
The the magic wouldn't stay around!
As I waited, not expecting one
The book of runes glowed like the sun!

I heard lilting music – of a lyre!
The moonlight, milk white, turned to fire
The breeze strode in, the pages turned
In the moonlight, fiery, bright lines burned

"A b-burning question, you have asked!"
I turned sharply, saw the strangest cast
Short, round, in a striped yellow suit
He stood next to me, oddly cute

A grin on his face, he held a lyre
Which didn't match his work attire
"Who are you, Sir?" I think I muttered
"Why, an angel, of c-course!" he stuttered

He looked divine of course, I could see
Looked as kind as "divine" could be
His rotund face had a beaming smile
Though he had a strange clothing style

The lyre, of course, I'd seen in books
But angels in books had special looks
They were slim and wore such lovely things
Like flowing garbs – and they had wings

This angel here wore a bright striped suit
Like a honey-bee's back, and strong boots
I wanted to know, but thought we must
Have this answer, absolutely, first

The angel seemed to read my mind
Reached the book, left his lyre behind
He read the runes like a fairy tale
By a bonfire on a camping trail

"Angels among us, of- oftentimes"
"Forget, and m- must return sometimes"
"To take wings like a b- butterfly"
"We wonder why, and so we c- cry"

As he closed the book, it did seem
That it had once belonged to him
"Let me now ex- explain each line"
"Jimmy is an angel, he'll be fine"

"After angels earn their b- bowstrings"
"They m- must stay and await their wings"
"But some forget – l- leave anyway"
"And have to be summoned right away"

"It's sad, I say," he said with a sigh
"Then they do make everyone c- cry!"
"For they must return – wings are k- key"
"But once they do, are happy and free!

"Jimmy was the best angel of all"
"If you saw his wings, you'd swoon and fall"
"He just *f- forgot*!!" He shook his head
"They wait for him" he grinned and said

The coon plucked the lyre, as if to play
For now, I didn't know what to say
Then I asked him, with some unease
"How do you know, Sir? Do tell me please"

"Ah! Well I, um, happened to b- be"
"In just this spot like your friend Jimmy"
He wiggled his toes inside his shoes
"I'm kind of an absent-minded muse!"

His voice, though often halted in flow
Had the gentle touch of driven snow
He wasn't well attired, as angels go
But had around a halo, a glow

It made me sad as I thought about
A world with Jimmy, a world without
"That's it!" He smiled "Now I must g- go"
"One more thing, Sir! Why are you dressed so?"

"These?" pointing to his striped pantaloon
He said, "I work for the Magical Moon"
"I t- tuck my wings, because those things"
C- cause......*Crash! Tinkle Clink Blink ...Zing...*

Interrupted by these sounds, and flash
He sighed, "That's a m- moonbeam crash!!"
"A wink I leave, and they c- collide"
"Just not *careful* when they d- drive!"

"Well, of c- course now I must g- go"
"I control t- traffic for the moon, 'nso"
Then with the friendliest, warm embrace
He was gone in a whiff, with no trace

For long we gazed, the coons and I
Through the window at the night sky
The stars hadn't gathered like before
There'd been a traffic jam, you know...

The little coon now held the lyre
And Mom coon looked at it with ire
He'd be scolded, being sure of that
"Next question!" I gave him a pat

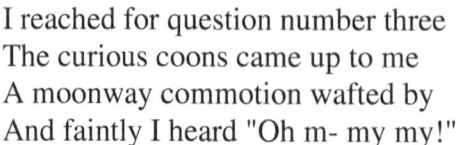

I reached for question number three
The curious coons came up to me
A moonway commotion wafted by
And faintly I heard "Oh m- my my!"

Transaction 5-4-3-2-1-2-4

MY THIRD question, a difficult one
Involved everyone under the sun
We're all the same, they said, *all* of us
No one minus, and no one plus

Yet in places near and far away
I'd seen such poor children at play
They had no shoes, and their clothes were torn
They lived on the streets from night to morn

This wouldn't be answered, I was sure
For my wording was rather obscure
"Why do some enjoy, others endure?"
Instead of why some are rich, some poor

The quivering lines rolled in a spool
Knotted up laughing, "Oh, what a fool!"
"How could one tell then, who were which?!"
"Why, some are poor so some can be rich!"

I suppose they made a point quite fine
With no gaps between, there'd be no line!
The pen, now glowing emerald green
Wrote my words firmly, stout and clean

Perfectly placed, their inky whorls
Now emerald runes with ruby swirls
Crimson for rich and green for poor
"What next?" I thought, rather unsure

In the flicker of a candle wick
The moonlight seemed to play a trick
The curtains fluttered high, aside
And I saw balloons bob up and glide!

I heard the clink of a falling coin
And a voice that said "Two ninety nine"
I leaned on the sill and peered outside
It was too bright for one to hide!

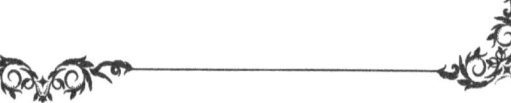

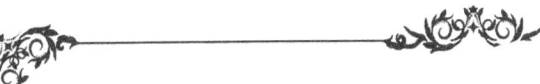

No one! And a car that wasn't mine!
Balloons on it with a "For Sale" sign
Puzzled, I turned back to the door
Saw a shiny gold coin on the floor!

I was flummoxed and wondered when
The curtains billowed once again
Gusts ruffled through the book of runes
Blew hot melodies, puffed cold tunes

Heated for rich and cold for poor?
I'd know soon! And know for sure
The magical moon sent in a ray
Like sunshine stolen from the day

It silvered up some burnished runes
Like a lantern placed beside festoons
Then I saw, sitting on the chair
A thin person with mousy hair!

His smile was broad as he looked at me
In a suit, hat, tie… Who could this be?
He said "Well hey! What do you know?"
Then "Five four three two one two four!"

With a buoyant, sharp look on his face
Reached the sill with a sprightly pace
"There's my car – its on sale today!"
"Priced two and ninety nine for today"

There I stood, positively floored
Like the coin I had so far, ignored
"Who are you Sir?" "Why'd you sell your car?"
"For just pennies in my penny jar!"

"And those numbers – what do they mean?"
"Was that the sound of a cash machine?"
"Well Well! So many questions! Whew!"
"But first, I'll read these runes to you"

Then pointing to the silvery lines
He began to read: "The wealth of times"
"Is built, and is not just happenstance"
"Like a game that one could win by chance"

"The poor are rich in what rich are poor"
"Its what we count, want or endure"
"Good hearts alone have often made"
"Those poor, rich of the richest grade"

"Low times, high tides sometimes do take"
"Riches and fortunes in their wake"
"As they rise and fall, wax and wane"
"Where castles stood, wet sands remain"

He closed the book and turned to me
Then clapped and counted "One two three…"
As he counted up to ten one way
With each, one line faded to gray

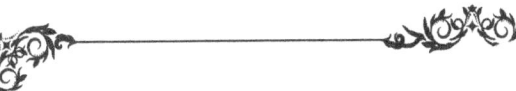

And then he uttered the strangest thing
"Come on! let's take my car for a swing!"
"Its such a magical night outside"
"Let's all go on for a jolly ride!"

The coons vigorously nodded "Yes!"
And no sooner had I said "Yes, let's"
We were in the car and headed out!!
I wondered what *this* was all about

Mom and Pop coons now sat in the back
And li'l coon snugly sat on his lap
In his pinstriped, impeccable style
He drove with precision, and a smile

"Let me first explain the one two three"
"For that, I normally charge a fee"
"All answers must be paid for, y'see"
"But yours have been paid for already"

"My name is Toby, how do you do?"
"Next question? – You had so many, phew!"
"Yes!" he said, "I sell refurbished cars"
"Although I'm a banker to the stars"

"I live quite close, by the starry style"
"On the isle you see – the Moonbeam Isle"
"Its reachable from the Bridge of Lune"
"On such nights of the magical moon"

"I was on audit today on Mars"
"(close of financials for the stars)"
"An insurance claim – some moonbeam crash"
"My cash register wouldn't open for cash"

"I pried it open, and all seemed fine"
"Until I found it missed one gold coin"
"Oh, Sir! I should've mentioned before"
"Was that your coin, on my attic floor?

"Why, Thanks! I'll look when we are back"
"Where was I? yes, it's my job to track"
"The expenses of the stars at large"
"I saw two debits tonight on charge"

"And ten pending, plus one transaction"
"For which expense is just a fraction"
The li'l coon glanced sideways at me
"Jimmy's – Five four three two one two three"

"And next," he said "is this one, you know"
"Transaction Five four three two one two four!"
"Your answer I'll explain in a while"
"As we cross the long bridge to the isle"

Soon on it, he began to explain
"Its all about balance, loss and gain"
"Everything nice can be cashed upon"
"Some don't know this, some are dead-on"

"Jane works hard but she does not know"
"Why she has so little wealth to show"
"She's rather plain, and not very smart"
"But she does have the kindest heart"

"She helps others, yet struggles so much"
"If she, while helping such and such"
"Just asked gently (not brazenly flat)"
"Would you do this if I helped with that?"

"Some would agree and some would not"
"Some could help and perhaps some not"
"But day by day, she'd very soon find"
"More for herself, while still being kind"

"She'd be richer in at least one way"
"She'd have more time to laugh and play"
"She'd have more time to do other things"
"And those could bring her riches on wings"

"Thanks!" I said, "but I don't understand"
"Why bad people get no reprimand"
"Oh they do cheat in different ways"
"But are not so fine most of their days"

"They gather riches till they are numb"
"Count them to a billion (and then some)"
"But they're not content, like you and me"
"Nothing we have – but nothing – is free"

"So don't compare, be good and learn"
"Riches you need aren't hard to earn"
"You'd be, helping others learn and grow"
"Richer, more cherished than you'd know"

"That's all to it, its more simple, see?"
"Than Five four three two one two three!!"
Suddenly a whistling gust blew in
I now glanced out – at a lovely scene!

The night was bright, like soft daylight
The Moonbeam isle gleamed green, blue, white
There, on the bridge, from far away
Came sounds of squeals, children at play

"Do you like this car?" He was blithe so
"Yes! But, Toby, why's the price so low?"
"In sales run by the Magical Moon"
"Prices are so low, some people swoon!"

"Moreover, this one was in a crash"
"Just yesterday – happened in a flash"
"Traffic angel left – emergency"
"This lost control, crashed into a tree"

"There's a dent on the right, as you see"
"It's refurbished (between you and me)"
"But its mileage is great – goes quite far"
"Gives ten more wishes per wishing star"

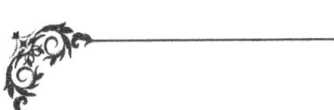

As Toby's car raced to Moonbeam Isle
It grew bright as daylight in a while!
"Its the picture! softly said Mom-coon
"It's Wysocki! gruffly said Dad-coon

In my attic hung, upon the wall
A picture, tacked with a poem small
I looked ahead with astonishment
The isle was the poem! And it went:

A bridge that spans two miles or three
Four lanes, two each approach and flee
Lead to an island five miles wide
Lively, bustling from side to side

So many odd forms, large and small
Side by side in a small town sprawl
Streetlights, trees, wagons and larks
Homes end-to-end, quaint shops and parks

A fence, a carriage, pumpkin stall
A horse, seagulls, and farmland sprawl
People, flags, parades and balloons
Tinsel, baubles, chintzy festoons

They all look lovely, vivid, bright
Like quilts laid out in the sunlight
Each object, in such sharp outline
Drawn in the finest sable line

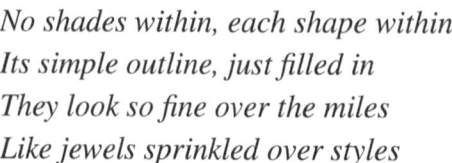

No shades within, each shape within
Its simple outline, just filled in
They look so fine over the miles
Like jewels sprinkled over styles

The sky azure, is clear and bright
Tendrils of smoke, puffs cotton-white
On rooftops drawn in gentle hand
Terracotta, gray, beige and sand

A child's painting, and yet it's not
A masterpiece of vivid thought
All these houses, the sky, the train
Each street here, a memory lane

A hundred quaint homes, bright and still
Like jewels scattered down a hill
On this canvas the world you see
Is a masterpiece - a Wysocki!

Qui dolorem ipsum quia dolor
We went around the town some more
On this delightful isle on which
Some were quite poor and some were rich

On the streets we saw horse carriages
Big mansions and some small cottages
When I mumbled, "No, I mustn't compare"
We were back! And Toby was still there!

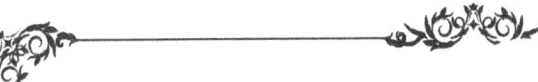

In his nimble hands he held a sheet
With an address "Moonbeam Isle, Third street"
"Toby's Used Cars," read the topmost line
The paper looked old, yellowed and fine

"A transfer of title, for used cars"
"Once you sign here, the car is yours!"
The car I liked – was magical too
And though it was used, it looked like new

I counted my coins: Two ninety nine
"Here you go, Sir, I hope that's fine"
The pen with a whoosh was on the line
Waiting poised on it for me sign!

When I did, with the broadest smile
He signed and stowed it in his file
Handed me some silver keys with wings
"Keep them all! They'll open many things"

I thought to ask, but a frazzled row
A traffic chase with the wind in tow
Stopped me, and he muttered, "I must go!"
"To meet another client, you know!"

"Is this your coin?" I reached for it
"Oh yes! It's lucky, so please keep it!"
"Thanks!" I said, but before I finished
With a whiff, he as gone, that was it!

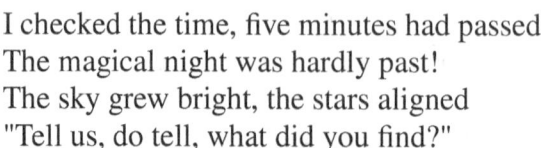

I checked the time, five minutes had passed
The magical night was hardly past!
The sky grew bright, the stars aligned
"Tell us, do tell, what did you find?"

Qui dolorem ipsum quia dolor
I told them why some were rich, some poor
Then I watched them slide away, disperse
Shine less or more in the universe

I reached for question number four
It looked just like the one before!
Its shine and sheen were all the same
And so was its constellation's name!

For I hadn't told you this before
That every star was called so-and-so
The third one's name had been Aldulfin
This one was Musica, its twin!

The Constellation

BEFORE I go to question four
I wonder if you'd want to know
The names of stars in that dancing row
Strange names that did entice me so

The brightest in the celestial town
Like a diamond in the night sky's crown
Had been Albaldah, the first in line
The second, Meissa, like bright sunshine

The twins Aldulfin and Musica were next
Brother and sister in celestial context
The fifth, Veritate, shone bright and true
The sixth was Electra, silver-blue

The seventh? Was it, oh, Aldebaran?
Alrakis, Alruba or Rastaban?
Lilii Borea? No, Mira! No, Dziban!
Alderamin, perhaps...Oh yes, Toliman!

The eighth star was named little Alco
Next, Deneb, with magpies in a row
A hundred ninety five magpies
With stolen jewels of the skies

The tenth star looked forlorn from afar
Was it Maia, Regulus or Izar?
Izar, I think. Regulus was next
A princely star, as often indexed

The twelfth was Spica, slightly green
Glowed with a bright translucent sheen
Across the sky its sprightly traipse
Like a happy gatherer of grapes

And the final star was called Altair
Soared high and low with an eagle's flair
Would be bright at first, then a distant streak
Like the light of Sirius, strong then weak

I knew such a question wouldn't stay
The moment asked, it would fly away
First flaring up, and then turning down
Cavorting so like a circus clown

Back to the questions, where were we?
Oh yes, on four, right after three
It would be, counting up from Toby's drive
Transaction Five four three two one two five

Transaction 5-4-3-2-1-2-5

A QUESTION that perplexed me so
Twin to the one I'd asked before
Why cannot some friends cope at school
Though they work hard, follow each rule

Why are some people just so smart
Some poor at lessons, from the start
Though they learn the very same things
Some fly ahead, like they have wings

As the pen wrote fast, scribbled this down
I saw Mom'n Pop coon nod and frown
The question seemed to cause concern
As if someone's homework wasn't done

The words, completed, didn't change
No runes appeared, 'twas rather strange
For a while they struggled on their path
Then turned to runes in chemistry, math!

With symbols and numeric strings
Elements, compounds, benzene rings
Functions, fractions, powers and roots
Exponents, graphs and attributes

On sheets of music, set to play
The symbols then began to sway
The breeze had tiptoed in, discreet
It strummed the symbols on that sheet

It sallied, surged and made a din
As the book lay quietly, wafer thin
Like crests of breaking waves of tide
Its pages welled now, milky white

Then a million pages rustled by
Invisible as the winds grew high
It seemed as if a wizard's hand
Now milled them into grains of sand!

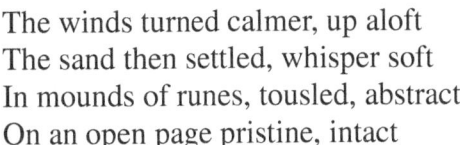

The winds turned calmer, up aloft
The sand then settled, whisper soft
In mounds of runes, tousled, abstract
On an open page pristine, intact

Burnished they looked, tan, beige and pink
A million runes in sparkling ink
They wavered at the wind's command
And moved around like shifting sand

I watched in dismay as they tossed
Was the answer to my question lost?
Who'd ever read these, or comprehend?
And if they could, would it ever end?

"Of course they can be read with ease!"
"Leave *that* to me now, if you please!"
Her commanding voice, strong as nails
Came wafting down the moonbeam trails

She walked down one, to the book
Wore a legal robe, a regal look
For a moment, I think, no one spoke
Was this Toby? Was this a joke?

If indeed this was Toby, then how
Was he prettier and shorter now?
"Herewith I read," she waved her hand
"The rulings of these grains of sand"

"This is *Article MM-pi-tau*"
"Also called *The Celestial Law*"
"Summarium, conlecto of all"
"Comprises your key, herewithall"

"Its provisions hereby I condense"
"This Celestial Law in one sentence"
"Each one shall (it's stipulations say)"
"Excel in minimum of one way"

She tossed her curls, a legal mane
"Celestial laws are quite germane"
"Each one meticulously writ"
"Examined and vetted to wit"

"These grains of sand are letters of law"
"In the finest prints you ever saw"
"Constantly updated, these runes"
"Consequently shift, like sandy dunes"

We thanked her, then so like Toby
"I'm Tory." She then said simply
"For now," she said, "I must interpret"
"And explain the answer you must get"

"Having processed, I conclude today"
"Upon this law that's on display"
"Not knowing their primum area"
"They beget no honoraria"

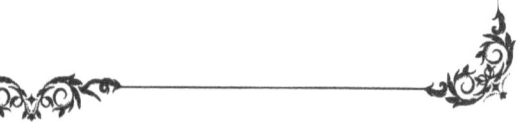

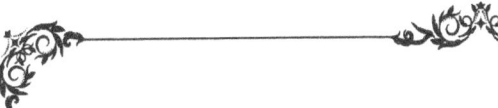

"If you pursued what you excel in"
"You'd rise like a tornado's spin"
"My surmise, as Attorney of Law:"
"It's what you choose, and not a flaw!"

"This book is a binding contract"
"Between two, as a matter of fact"
"Magic and you, witnessed by those"
"Stars in the constellation you chose"

"If you ask *why*, in its purview"
"No answer shall be owed to you"
"Once obtained, be it dense or sparse"
"A true account is owed to the stars"

We listened to this in reverence
Said in the past participle tense
Tori looked benevolent as rain
"I must go!" Tossed her legal mane

I thanked her, but wished I knew
Why she said this like Toby too
Almost on cue, she said on her own
"He's my twin brother," in a bright tone

"He spoke of you, so I had to see"
"And besides, this answer had to be"
"Condensed by someone legally"
"Into to a concise summary"

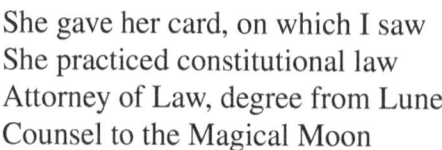

She gave her card, on which I saw
She practiced constitutional law
Attorney of Law, degree from Lune
Counsel to the Magical Moon

Looking up again – no one there!
One star winked like a solitaire
The other stars, from the moonlit sky
Were a tad behind, I wondered why

Oh! The answer still wasn't complete!
I remembered how the lines, replete
With symbols in their rune-filled path
Had puzzled me – why they'd had math!

Then I realized, as once before
That I just liked chemistry more
Did well in math, but was behind
In other subjects of that kind

I mentioned this to the solitaire
Waiting until all stars were there
They then dispersed to shine away
Each one so special in its way

The next bright question in the row
Twinkled, brilliant, ready to go
There was a soft poke at my shoe
The coon wanted it answered too!

The Harlequin

THE FIFTH question was old, not new
It wasn't straight, had a twist, a skew
An elusive, tricky one to ask
A harlequin in a second mask

I closed my eyes, a moment paused
The question then aloud I tossed
The pen was poised upon the lines
That had tangled over many times!

My question touched on warring tribes
Conflicted homes and angry vibes
On friends and foes and acts of war
On the weapons of the Alcazar

"Why is there strife, why are there wars?"
"On this lovely planet Earth of ours?"
"Why do people fight, near and far?"
"Why are we divided as we are?"

"All things around exist in peace"
"We share the sky, the sun, the seas"
"Flowers, mountains, meadows, trees"
"Moonlight, starlight, grass and breeze"

"Rivers, clouds, the beautiful rain"
"All things to everyone, germane"
"Why do they fight then? Tell me why!"
The curtains fluttered with a sigh

The pen was still, and hadn't moved
For my question was a little skewed
I wondered how the pen could write
On warring lines that cross, divide

On that starry night, clear and warm
Came the rumble of a thunderstorm
I heard a sound, a crash, a boom
Felt a spray of rain inside the room!

The lines were knotted, jumbled up
A strange gray cloud now tumbled up
A thunderbolt was in its tone
The reason for its wrath unknown

Perhaps it looked, its manner told,
For lightning missing from its fold
With dark demeanor, grim intent
It rained on lines 'til they unbent

I wondered what this was about
This seemed to be a cloud of doubt
The lines hung straight like mousy hair
The coons had climbed up on the chair

I wasn't drenched, though in a daze
The pen scrolled through the straightened maze
My question set wet lines ablaze
They had smoky runes, under a haze!!

A squall came in, blew magic tunes
Turned pages of the book of runes
As the burning question grew more charred
A page opened, underlined and starred

Moonbeams rushed in then, with a flash
Their glow ignited, like whiplash
Dark smoke arose, and when it cleared
Left smoldering runes, sooty and smeared

A voice rang out "Then there was smoke"
"They looked for fire in woods of oak"
"In those woods, there were mystic things"
"Castles of storms, in magic rings"

"Eerie places and leprechauns"
"Witch cottages and strange flying forms"
"No fire was found, and will never be"
"For the flames were of disharmony"

My heart beat fast, my breath was cold
The coons hid in the curtain's fold
"Who are you Sir?" I asked, terrified...
"A harlequin" the voice replied

A strobe of moonlight through the pall
Circled a shadow by the wall
Like a soldier figurine, of tin
There he stood upright: a Harlequin!

Who was this gallant? I feared to ask
On his face he wore a paper mask
His red-gold costume, top to toe
Had little stars that sparkled so

His costume tapered at his wrists
In triangular strips and twists
Down to his ankles and his hips
His shoes were curled up at their tips

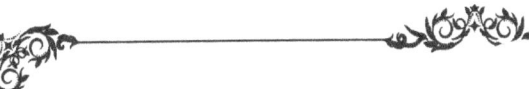

In diamond motif, little bells
Sewn on his costume, tinkled spells
Each time he moved, they'd softly sing
Some new enchanted choral string

Sounds like you may have never heard
As if all notes had been shattered
Recomposed into sprays of rain
And sand grains blown across a plain

Although we couldn't see his face
His melodies, gestures and grace
His tone, his words, his smiling voice
Implied he was gentle and nice

"Please! Do not be afraid of me!"
"I'm just a harlequin, you see"
"A different one – clown nor buffoon"
"Strategist for the Magical Moon"

Like shadows on a moonlit night
That vanish at the break of light
I felt my panic, fear, suspense
Just disappear, and I wasn't tense

He gently shut the book of runes
With that, bells struck enchanted tunes
The same ones, of a summer brook
That had first opened the magic book!

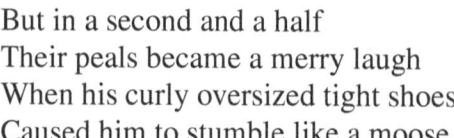

But in a second and a half
Their peals became a merry laugh
When his curly oversized tight shoes
Caused him to stumble like a moose

Before they had a chance to quell
He tripped again and almost fell!
The bells then spiraled to his cue
As he spun upright like corkscrew

I really would have never known
Until this incident had shown
How a true strategist's fall and rise
Could so completely mesmerize

"Your answer," he said, "is best told"
"By the actors in the Dance of Wold"
"Its about to open very soon"
"In ballrooms of the Magical Moon"

I began a question: "But how could..."
And lo and behold – I found we stood
In a hall of such splendor, grandeur
With stardust sprinkled on the floor

The hall was decked with strands and rays
Of moonlight, starlight, sunny days
And with "M.M.A.U." tagged on them,
Were flowers, each a fragrant gem

I wondered what those letters meant
They seemed to be faintly portent
But then, just as the music rose
For then, I stopped thinking of those

He waved his hand, his fingers fanned
Conjured an invisible band
Slender, lithe forms moved to the floor
A hundred dancers, maybe more

The dance began, a glorious sight
A Masque, of beauty and delight
A hundred forms moved daintily
With the music, in such harmony

How could a dance of such accord
Explain the reasons for discord?
How could a whole answer exist
In the midst of operatic grist?

We'd soon see how it did exist
Why he was a master strategist
Why he had to show with such ado
An answer that he clearly knew

Throughout, the harlequin controlled
The dance, with such powers untold
It seemed he was its overseer
Its mastermind, its puppeteer

In this choreographed dance they wore
Masks and unique costumes galore
Each different, so they'd recognize
With whom they had to harmonize

The harlequin said softly "Watch!"
The music now went down a notch
He raised an arm in a sweeping spin
And each form became a harlequin!

It was a strange sight to behold
For all those harlequins of Wold
With masks, now couldn't recognize
With who they had to harmonize

The choreographed sequence then broke
Some stopped, as notes began to choke
Then as angry notes began to rise
The harlequin gave his surmise:

"When we pretend, hide our true selves"
"When we pretend we're someone else"
"Our acts, cloaked in costumes of lies"
"Break harmony, conflicts arise"

With a graceful gesture he invoked
A spell that instantly revoked
The warmth and comfort in the hall
To a little spot between them all

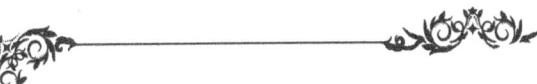

The dancers broke their rhythmic pace
Approached the spot that had no space
And there under the blazing lights
Rose arguments, struggles and fights

"Unfulfilled wants, and sometimes greed"
"Are reasons for so much misdeed"
He gestured, and his magic bells
Restored the ambiance, with spells

The dance went on, a winsome sight
The dancers sparkling, jaunty, bright
I wondered, through its soft murmur
Where they lived and who they were

The harlequin – the mask he wore
Seemed then to smile a little more
"They're students from the School of Lune"
"A province of the Magical Moon"

"The School of Lune has twenty parts"
"Of which one is Performing Arts"
"It's a distinguished academy"
"Of the M.M. University"

I was startled how he read my mind
I couldn't comprehend his kind
As I wondered, silent all the while
On his mask appeared a broader smile

"A final thing I shall explain"
"And leave your answer to remain"
"A thought to think, a muse to muse"
"To observe keenly, a good excuse"

With a sweep, the dancers changed again
In groups they glittered, or were plain
The dance then very slowly changed
The dancers steps now rearranged

Each group went to a different side
Between them was a great divide
"They've only learned to dance beside"
"Costumes, and not with those inside!"

"Their leaders, teachers must now guide"
"How they must dance with no divide"
"To clear *their* clouds of doubts, and mists"
"We have (yours truly) strategists"

As he said this, in a flash of light
We were in my attic's soft moonlight
And there lay rolling on the floor
A glittering mask, beside the door!

I looked at it, quite astonished
It was a thought I had dismissed
It was a dancer's, who had been
Of great composure through the scene

I realized, as in times before
As I looked down at my attic floor
That the hall could have been, very well
An artifact of a magic spell!

"I must leave now," as he turned to go
I thanked him, but I had to know...
"Who are you Sir, under that mask?"
An impertinent question to ask...

"A strategist...to the Magical Moon!"
He sang with all his bells in tune
"Does this satisfy you?" he then asked
And removed his mask – but was still masked!

He removed that too, without a word
But beneath the second, was a third!
"I'm sorry Sir, I did intrude"
"Do accept my sincere gratitude"

"My pleasure!" came his warm reply
Like the embrace of a fond goodbye
With that, his moonlit form, outlined
Faded to a shadow, left behind

We stood silent on the attic floor
Three masks remained, one by the door
There, in the sigh of a wistful gust
I caught a glint of fine stardust

The book of runes, its pages gray
Like the harlequin, faded away
The stars of Wold came waltzing through
When told the answer, off they flew

And for a while, the coons and I
Gazed at the stars, then waved goodbye
Brewing like a mellow wine
Question six was next in line

Aflatoon

QUESTION SIX was a simple one
Light, though its answer weighed a ton
No, the answer wasn't short or thin
Was round, like a Pundit or a Djinn

As I reached for Electra, silver-blue
It warmed up to an orange hue
Like a winter morning, chill and cold
Warms to sunshine, turns to gold

I heard a footstep! And then more
And Tommy peeped in through the door!
"Tommy! Look! How did you get here?
His excited eyes shone bright and clear

"I saw lights in your attic, all a-glow"
"Saw balloons, and birds fly in a row"
"Heard a crash in your driveway, saw a car"
"I *had* to come, and your door was ajar. . ."

I told him all, then paused somewhat
We stood in silence, deep in thought
A little bird by the window, said
Tweetingly, "Shall I ask instead?"

"Oh, no, but thank you little bird!"
Then I framed clearly, word for word:
"Why do we grow up, and grow old?"
"When as children we are good as gold"

The pen drew bows and ponytails
Made paper ships with paper sails
With words it wrote, along the trails
Of lines that ran like railroad rails

The words then turned in single file
Into runes that looked so juvenile
But turned to youth of great allure
That soon grew somber and mature

The breeze crooned up a song sublime
That started as a nursery rhyme
That Mom coon softly hummed along
The magic book stirred to the song

For a moment then it opened wide
The pages blew from side to side
Like the soft hairs of a stallion's mane
But the magic book then shut again!

Then it didn't open as before
Perhaps it was waiting for some more?
Or someone who, on this full moon
Knew which page to open to the tune

Whoosh! Then we heard a swishing sound
Lo and behold! We suddenly found
On a flattened chair, a heavy Djinn
Who stood up muttering "Flimsy tin..."

Then said "Hel-llo! Marhaba dear all!"
"I arrive on time, desbite the stall"
"My – er – lamb had sprung a tiny leak"
"That makes its sbell a little weak!"

"What do we have here in this book?"
"By the way, new turban, how do I look?"
"What a difficult question, Oh, ho ho!!!"
"Nice," he muttered, "confusing, though..."

From his strange shoes, this amazing man
To his turban-top, spread like a fan
Was quite imposing, large and tall
He was round, and sturdy as a wall

His turban, jeweled, peachish gold
Had flecks of blue in its clever fold
From top to toe, he was dressed in silk
Wore a shiny vest, white as milk

Rings on all fingers, a creaky boot
With curly tips, of leather and jute
He wore necklaces, bracelets and blings
White and rose-pink pearly strings

He looked so funny in every way
What was to come, it was hard to say
For a moment we stood petrified
Then he spoke, perplexed but dignified

"Now to read...haven't done this before"
"I'm supposed to read some kind of lore"
"Well...," said I, "They may not be lores"
"You see that book?" and he said "Of course!"

"Although it looks so frail and thin"
"A million pages lie within"
"On one of those, some lines of runes"
"Answer the question in these tunes"

He scratched his ear with a thoughtful look
Tapped a pudgy finger on the book
We heard him grumble, and mutter
"And it won't oben?" I said "No Sir!"

He knit his brows, "Well, let me see"
"Not my line..." he clarified to me
He flipped open the magic book
With a rather miffed and bothered look

"Ahem," he said, and some lines lit up!
Over which he pored, his brows knit up
At first his face looked quite bemused
Then looked perplexed, then quite confused

"These words are written left to right!"
"Berhabs I should turn the book ubright!"
Whereupon he grumbled, "They're still wrong!"
"They're right from left still strung along"

From the right he read in a low hum
"Rhyme or reason need not do things some"
He paused and scratched the side of his face
Whistled a tune, stared into space

"Er... let's read from left to right this time"
"Some things don't need reason or rhyme"
"This makes sense! Aha!" Then he said
"That's quite simble!" And Bobbed his head

Here is how he explained, like a sage
The gist of words on the magic page:
"That's the way it is, for what it's worth"
"We're made of stuff, and live on earth"

Quite confused, and amused this time
We didn't ask for reason or rhyme
This genial genie, king of cartoons
Turned topside-down the book of runes

Pondered the words, thinking how they might
Be strung right to left, not left to right
When it didn't work, he turned it askew
Just thumbed its million pages through

As he hummed and poked, there was a whiff
A cloud passed by, and the book turned stiff
"Bah!" he exclaimed, on the chair he sat
Which collapsed promptly, again went flat

As he sat on the floor, with some grace
Moonbeams danced in, shone on his face
Then he demanded from where he was
"What's the time? Do you have an hourglass?"

"Er...no..." Sir, "But I do have a clock"
"That one?" He pointed, "Does it talk?"
"Talk? Well, um...er...I'd say, no..."
"Well, how will it tell when I must go?"

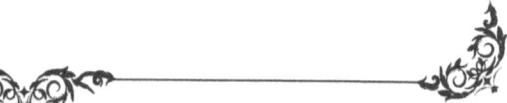

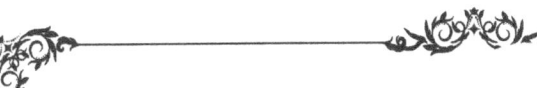

"Er...," said I, as he studied the chair
"Could I ask..." as he fixed it with flair
"Of course! What do you desire to know?"
"Um, when you go home, *where* do you go?"

I write this with such fond memory
Of the words that he then said to me
A loving soul, I'd say this twice
His words were so endearingly nice:

I'm a genie and my name is Aflatoon
I'm an area assistant to the Magical Moon
I serve a desert that's very far away
(It has lots of sand, and is hot in the day)
So far, that it took me a minute or two
To arrive in your attic to read to you
Your area assistant isn't here today
To read all the answers that are sent your way

Anyway

I live on a green oasis in the sand
Its full of flowers, and I own the whole land
It has the bluest lake you might've ever seen
It has balm trees, and melon fields, lush and green
So the moon asked me to fill in for the bart
But lines in your book are written end-to-start!

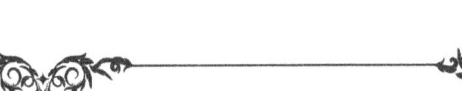

Anyway

Though the desert's full of sand, and it is large
I'm a genie, I can turn any mirage
Green and cool, so I'm embloyed for that bart
I serve those who wander, but are good at heart
Though these lines look all the same, and words the same
They do solve every buzzle that you could name

Anyway

I build castles of sand, or castles of clay
For the tired to rest after a weary day
Every once so often the Magical Moon
Sends me to read answers from some book of runes
But books in the desert, I know inside out
All of them read right to left, without a doubt

Anyway

In the day I relax, with hobbies and friends
Hawks and camels, and I make bottery blends
We laugh and joke, and blay very many games
Like Hide-and-Seek, Tab-Tab and Give-Me-Names
Sometimes I fill for some assistants as well
But I already said that, didn't I? Oh well!

Anyway ...

"Er... Sir, your description is rather confused"
"The last two lines aren't consistently used"
"Confused, was I?" he sighed "Oh dear!"
"I thought what I said was very clear"

"Would you say, at least, in your review"
"I also read from the left to you?"
"We are not confused, and it wasn't queer!"
"It was," said Tommy, "quite almost clear"

He beamed and his face lit like the moon
"I leave," he said "but will see you soon"
Then he counted through to twenty two
In a language that sounded quite new

But his spell went wrong, as it was said
For he hummed it left to right instead
The night grew cool, there was no sound
Then there were sand dunes all around!

On that clear and cold moonlit night
The ground was shifty, cushy, white
For miles around till everywhere
Just white cool sand – all that was there

"Oh dear! Oh my! Oh such a delight!"
He looked sheepish, fussed, apologized
Then happily he said "You're my guests"
Then worried, he said "But you must rest"

"A night here must be restfully spent"
Poof... Aflatoon created a tent
For tonight he didn't trust his spell
By daylight he thought all might be well...

Everything we asked for just appeared
With his gesture, or it disappeared
"Aikhtafaa!" he would say with a smile
And wave his pudgy hands in style

When morning dawned, still cold and bright
Outside on the dunes, still endless, white
Were marks of letters, over the sand
A spell practiced by a pudgy hand!

Aflatoon said, with a beaming smile
"And now, my friends," waved his hands in style
Lo and behold! There a hummingbird
In the beautiful oasis, now appeared!

Lush, fragrant plants grew all around
Water lapped to a soothing sound
Gardens, lawns and among them all
Stood lovely homes, both large and small

Beyond them was a magical sight!
A beautiful palace, brilliant white
Tall spires topped with the moon and stars
Its walls had vines that scrolled memoirs

He pointed, said "That one, do you see?"
"Is my palace where we shall soon be!"
Then he hummed something, gestured wide
And lo and behold, we stood inside!

There, with marble arcades all around
Halls with mirrors, rugs, incense and sound
Was an open courtyard, paved in plaid
Its walls were bougainvillea clad

Lined with trees, under silk hammocks
Roamed a lovely posse of peacocks
In the courtyard stood a banyan tree
Underneath, a man with white goatee

Dressed like a saint, he was quite intent
On instructing players, who were bent
Studiously on a game of dice
"Tamash Bin..." he said, "He's very wise!"

"He's Instructor of the Games, you see"
"For every lock, he has the key"
"A game of chance is tough, you know"
"You *have* to practice, to be a pro"

The players practiced throwing dice
Coached by Tamash Bin, sage and wise
Everything was curious, had strange names
We met his friends and played some games

"You must also meet" said Aflatoon
With pride and joy, "my pet platoon"
This is as far as I can go
What ensued next is described below:

Standing in a row
Looking down in contempt
Their beautiful eyes
Rather intent
His camel friends
In the finest attire
Contemplated the world
Like birds on a wire
His hawks whereas
Sat high on the wall
Pretending to be camels
As strong, more tall
Shrugging their wings
Preening and proud
Nonchalantly looked
At this plebeian crowd

At the far end roamed
A ferocious leopard
Didn't care to be a camel
Or even a bird
Aflatoon called to it
No movement ensued
He said "Come to me!"
The leopard stood glued
His expression, of disdain
Said "I'm not in the mood"
The coon, now curious
Poked his nose from behind
He'd been hiding at the back
From leopardkind
All at once with a roar
The spotted freak
Went after the coon
Like a lightning streak
"Bah" said a camel
"What peasants!" said a hawk
By the grass, royal goats
Refused to talk
They went round and round
In a blur, trill, roar
With a sigh Aflatoon
Said "Excuse this uproar..."

Reached out at the streak
As it speedily passed
Pinned under his arm
The leopard, quiet at last
Aflatoon scolded him
And he hung his tail
Which the coon promptly bit
And he gave a wail
Then a rumbling growl
"You – I'll quarter and impale!"
"And I'll send your parts"
"By celestial mail"

"That's enough!" said Aflatoon
"You're grounded for today!"
"Is this how we treat our guests?"
"What will everyone say?"
As the leopard slinked away
"He's Ibn," said Aflatoon
"He was stranded in a forest"
"In a land called Rangoon"
"They left him in a cage"
"They'd have set him free"
"He wasn't who they wanted"
"But a coon stole the key"

"I found him so next day"
"When the Magical Moon"
"On a temborary assignment"
"Sent me to Rangoon"

Across from the wall
Was an emerald lagoon
Crystal clear waters
More of his platoon
Peach pink flamingos
The camels of the seas
Lining the lagoon
Were grasses and trees
Many flowered bushes
Fragrances of June
"My favorite one"
"Is that bush called Jaitoon"
Parakeets chatted
There were so many around
As were frolicking foxes
On the far side ground

We went across to the great lagoon
To which we were led by Aflatoon
We soon set sail, seated aloft
A raft of wingwood, feather soft

For a moment, as the evening wore
The raft felt like my attic floor
Rippling gray-violet-green across
Was an incense field, like smoky moss

A field of nightlights flickered bright
With leaves like flames of candlelight
Silver fields swayed by the lagoon
"They're crobs of mirages," said Aflatoon

A cloudy field swirled dark and gray
"We grow thunder there," we heard him say
Faraway were some charming chalets
"There live my friends from childhood days"

As dusk fell, we just had to return
For question six wasn't really done
With a hug and wave, promise to meet
He read a spell, right to left from a sheet

I felt a cool wind in my hair
A gentle swoosh of desert air
And the raft became a rug and lay
On my attic floor, in its old way!

We sat in silence, rather stunned
So smoothly had we been returned
The book of runes lay thin and light
Its top side down, and left side right

Like the flurry of a sudden storm
The stars now gathered in a swarm
They asked what Aflatoon had said
I explained it in my words instead

Then they dispersed, some faint some bold
Some old, some new, some young, some old
Like firework or a lightning charge
A burst of sparks, some small some large

They sparkled, spread out far and wide
Shone nodding, twinkling, satisfied
And now was time for the next prelude
For the magical moon's interlude

"Can I ask one?" sounding breathless, rushed
Tommy asked, with his face quite flushed
"Dear Tommy, yes of course, you know"
"Ask the top one in that starry row"

He gripped my hand then, very tight
"Just read, and the magic pen will write!"
And so he picked up after mine
The seventh question in the line

The Agricultural Scholar

THE SEVENTH one, not quite like those
I'd asked before, because the rows
Had changed to Tommy's ones for now
It was rather nice of them, somehow

The breeze was warm, set up a croon
I was glad to share the magical moon
I was glad to have my friends with me
The greatest magic there could be

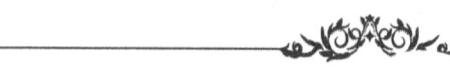

Like drumrolls in breathless serfage
Of curtains as they're drawn on stage
The pen was poised, hovered about
The lines were smooth and straightened out

They looked like furrows in a field
Through which a plower had been wheeled
"Why won't my new tomatoes grow?"
The pen wrote with a crimson glow

The words now on the topmost line
Became a dazzling plant, a vine
With soft green leaves and round red fruits
Which, below the underline, had roots!

Through them now blew a zesty breeze
Billowed, smoothed the curtain's crease
Then set the magic book upright
(Aflatoon had flipped it left-top-side)

The breeze now hummed a rustic tune
The coons began a country croon
The pages were a block of gray
As though composed of earth and clay

The answer surely was to come
The ashen clay changed with the hum
And to the croon of village streets
The book filled with a million sheets

Flapping in the breeze, it's sighs
Sounded like wings of butterflies
It's pages in accordion's fold
Riffled back silver, and forth gold

Of a million pages, one it chose
With fields and hay, gardens of rose
Which then lay open, calm and still
With runes like wheatfields by a mill

From the window, came in white moonlight
Set two rippling rows of wheat alight
Tommy exclaimed "What do they say?"
"Hush!" "We can't read wheat anyway!"

"I know what's written there by heart!"
We heard suddenly, with a start
"This is *the* one, I'm sure of that!"
"So much dust!" then a pat-pat-pat

"A Magnum Opus" said the voice
"To languish thus! Hope not by choice..."
In the attic, now lit milky white
There seemed to be no one in sight

A plop at the window! What was it?
It was an owl! "To-woo! To-wit!"
"An owl!" said Tommy "That's absurd"
"That can't be just a silly bird!"

"Now, let's see...," we whirled around
The source of the sonorous sound!
A slim young man, in spectacles
Clutching such sundry articles

Not too tall, by his side a bag
'M.M.A.U.' printed on its tag
Pen in pocket, ruler and a note
On which all salient points he wrote

In his hand he held a dusty book
On his face was a studious look
He peered down at a glowing line
His hair fell forward, straight and fine

"How pulchritudinous!" Said he"
"This paper is extraordinary!"
"This volume must absolutely be"
"From the Magical Moon's library!"

"But first, indeed, I must proceed"
"Scarcely a duo of lines to read..."
"Subsequenty, I shall explain"
"Their gist, in words extremely plain"

I stifled a laugh, the owl a twit
Tommy stifled a giggling fit
"Of purest heart, sunshine of love"
"The seeds of deeds will be a grove"

He cleared his throat, consulted his book
Then with a grave, scholarly look
Began to explain, and this is how:
"My esteemed colleagues, allow me now"

"To demonstrate an optimum yield"
He clapped, and we stood in a field!
Under a starry blue-gray sky
A field awash in blue-gray dye

He continued with much delight
Waved his hands in the bright moonlight
"Pay attention, please, as I explain"
Then he clapped his hands, twice again

The night instantly turned to dawn
Replete with colors of the morn!
The twitter of birds, skyward bound
The warmth of sunshine all around

The morning sky turned to afternoon
In it still shone the magical moon!
The fields of shades unknown turned green
For miles around, a wondrous scene

Most marvelous trees that ever grew
The sweetest smells you ever knew
The queerest fields beneath the blue
A magical land, through and through!

Rare blooms and grasses intertwined
Plants in ballet lines, aligned
Flourishing bushes and feathered trees
Cotton squashes and crystal reeds

"I now introduce you, dear colleagues"
"To my school, one of our Ivy Leagues"
"Of agriculture, and all its codes"
"I teach here, my name is Siebel Rhodes"

"From harvest moon to the spring commune"
"I consult for the Magical Moon"
"Now, as to our subject – the handsome"
"Plant, Solanum Lycopersicum"

"If you allow me, there you can see"
"Some that grow in the shade of that tree"
"Whereas those around are large and tall"
"Those in shade are obviously small"

"Plants grow resilient in sunlight's way"
"If properly hydrated each day"
"Observe – beyond those batches of plum"
"Are our groves of Lycopersicum"

They looked like pumpkins! Orange, maroon
Those tomatoes of the harvest moon!
"They are new, the latest on trial"
"Quite successful on celestial soil"

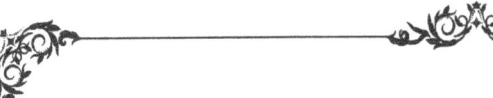

"Thus in answer to you, my dear Sir"
"Plants need water, sunlight and manure"
"And while you're here, in that barn you see"
"Are samples you can take back with ye"

Right across two fields of cotton yarn
By a farmhouse, was a wooden barn
The coon had questions, Tommy too
Many to ask, between me and you

"I will address further queries now"
He seemed to read our minds, somehow
So we asked about all things we saw
And he answered us with such éclat!"

Then Tommy said, "Please... er... may we"
"See some of your University?"
Siebel nodded, "Of course, of course!"
"*And* you may attend my class on Gorse!"

Around the school were yellow blooms
A sprawling compound, large classrooms
It was Siebel's class, in which sat
Some thirty students, and a brat

Here's his lecture: I only wrote
Some selected points, on my note
He taught for an hour, by the clock
On a blackboard with a squeaky chalk

GORSE <u>he</u> wrote with an underline
His expression neutral and benign
And just to make a point more fine
Below it, he drew a second line

Gorse is the plant, which you will see
In our west field number twenty three
I will begin (he wrote a b c)
With its requisite taxonomy
Then <u>Kingdom:</u>, <u>Phylum:</u>, <u>Class:</u>, he wrote
On the far left side of the board
Below these, <u>Order:</u>, like an ode
With <u>Family:</u>, his expression glowed

From the first term, he respectively
Wrote "Plantae" first, quite carefully
"Tracheophyta," with considerable glee
"Magnoliopsida," then, diligently
"Fabales," he wrote, subsequently
Against <u>Family:</u>, he finally
Scrolled down the word "Fabaceae"
And continued, eventually

<u>Genus:</u> "Ulex," <u>Species:</u> "Various"
"Gallii," "Densus," "Europaeus"
"Minor," "Aerensi," "Micranthus"
"And then we have the "Argenteus"

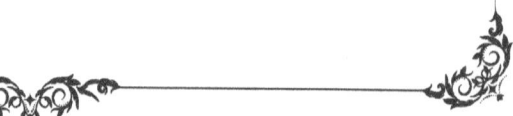

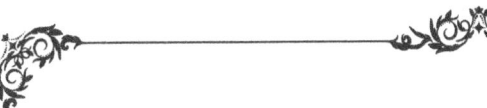

"With regard to those that grow with us"
"The species becomes "Celestius"
"The latter, now we will discuss"
<"What boring taxonomic fuss!">

"The prickliest shrub you can find"
<"He drives me clean out of my mind">
A whisper from the nether row
From a student, who we didn't know

"Its yellow flowers, needle leaves"
"Approximately appear like these"
He drew the shrub and flowers too
<"That looks like a kangaroo!">
"This species is a flowering shrub"
<"I'm drowning, help me! Blub blub blub...!">

. . .

Then he launched into a monotone
On how celestial gorse is grown

"Its usually planted as a seed"
"But its stalks do grow if they are freed"
"If it doesn't face the sun it mopes"
*"So you **must** grow it on mountain slopes"*

"Formula two in your textbook"
"Gives the shrub a translucent look"
"You must water it each day until"
"Each spine turns to a soft tendril"

. . .

"Its roots must be well chanted to"
"For it to walk and talk to you"
"Must be sprinkled at least twice with dew"
"Each day for it to look like new"

. . .

"When the yellow flowers turn to gold"
"Spell number twelve will then unfold"
"Their pink and peacock parchment wings"
"And then spell number thirteen brings"
"A breeze on which they fly around"
"To scatter seeds over the ground"

. . .

"...Grandma Muse's bedtime croon"
"Makes them bloom on a magical moon"

. . .

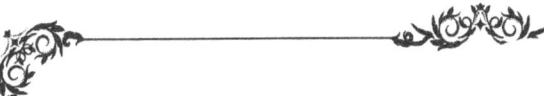

<"Oh my goodness, what a colossal bore!">
From the back bench came the loudest snore
A flying chalk, and then an "Ouch!"
A scolding, and a sullen slouch
A pesky snort, a grumbling tone
An imposition, to atone
Written on the board, quite an impasse
"I will not hereby comment in class"

...

He advanced to Gorse's history
Then expounded its phytology
Informed the class nonchalantly
That the next class would be "Berry Tree"
After an hour of this litany
I think everyone wanted to flee
I wasn't sure if I'd want to be
A professor in a university

Like a beeswarm irked from a hive
They buzzed outside at the strike of five
The pesky imp in passing said
<"Be afraid! Be full of dread!">

Siebel smiled, "please pay no heed"
"He's a pesky un, but helps in need"
"A difficult one he is, indeed"
"But in Taxonomy, takes the lead!"

Now we shall see our produce barn
It has all – from honey to yarn
It exhibits our latest yields
The newest produce from our fields

Most are here for culinary use
Its the favorite haunt of Grandma Muse
Even that (snotty) chef of Aflatoon
Likes the kitchen gardens of the moon

There are some departments we shan't see
E.g. the Great Harvest Faculty
They curate Autumn's harvest day
Keep accounts of (even) bales of hay

And the School of Orchards oversees
The counts of fruits on orchard trees
Each season they are modified
Their colors, tastes are all revised

But of course, you must really see
Our great produce inventory
The moonstone paths through magic fields
Led to this barn with magical yields

It was made of some celestial wood
Fragrant like myrrh and sandalwood
With a touch of cedar and brown oak
Had a cloud-roof like palmyra smoke

It had cherry doors, that opened wide
What treasures did we find inside!
The coon's bushel had tiny things
Like fairy figs with silky wings

We filled our bushels, one for each
With moon-white grapes, celestial peach
Squall nuts, canapes, bluegrass leaves
Parchment flowers in gossamer weaves

In awe, we thanked Siebel Rhodes
Litterateur of Botanical Codes
"Goodbye, colleagues, be right as rain"
"And very soon, we shall meet again"

A cloud passed by, for a moment then
We stood in the attic, once again
We gazed at the sky, and wondered so
What land had that been, we'd never know

The book of runes, now closed, was still
At my window, stars began to mill
Like Solanum grows on sunlit plains
Like Siebel's students' loud complaints

The stars stood there eager to know
The answer – Tommy told them so
They questioned us then, how and why
And then dispersed into the sky

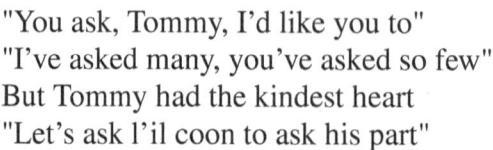

"You ask, Tommy, I'd like you to"
"I've asked many, you've asked so few"
But Tommy had the kindest heart
"Let's ask l'il coon to ask his part"

"Would you like to ask a question now?"
The coon eyes shone, he nodded his snout
He found his question star to read
His question was quite blunt, indeed!

City of Thieves

QUESTION EIGHT, asked by the coon
Was cute as the frown of Aflatoon
Fetched by the coon, it was then read
Aloud by Tommy, in his stead

The quivering lines began to laugh
An owl hooted a scornful scoff
The coon studied the attic floor
Sporting a pout, facing the door

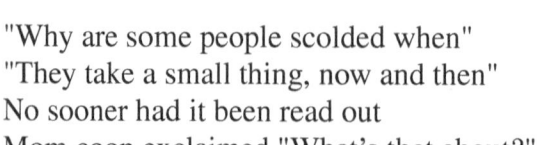

"Why are some people scolded when"
"They take a small thing, now and then"
No sooner had it been read out
Mom coon exclaimed "What's that about?"

"What sort of question is that, huh?"
"How often have I told you, huh?"
"To Steal is wrong! Must you remain"
"Impertinent and ask *again*?"

Dad coon stood sporting quite a frown
The pen moved swiftly, wrote it down
When cracked-up, swooping like a bird
A line criss-crossed and stole a word!

The question now was not complete
Though the perfect writing was replete
With pretty words aligned on lines
Like leaves arranged on climbing vines

With a whimper fell a tiny tear
The little coon looked sadly dear
The line uncrossed itself with grace
And left the missing word in place

Soon runes appeared like buildings strewn
In the bustle of an afternoon
Through a city drawn in great detail
The lines looked like a paper trail

The breeze then whistled up a jazz
Like busy downtown razzmatazz
The book of runes looked ordinary
Like an old telephone directory!

Its ruffling pages did quite look
Like someone searched an address book
And then it seemed, an address found
The book, left open, lay around

Like torchlight in a dark alley
Like a spotlight roving patiently
A moonbeam lit, as if on stage
An address on the smokey page

"Eight ninety nine!" announced a voice
Was strong but gentle, gruff but nice
But there was no one we could see
Whose voice was this? Who could it be?

Beside the window, then we spied
A person, who looked occupied
A rather stern, imposing man
Tall and broad, with a brown suntan

He wore a blue and black uniform
Held a lens and counted up a storm
"Nine thousand steps, nine thousand two"
"Nine thousand four... Wups! What have you?"

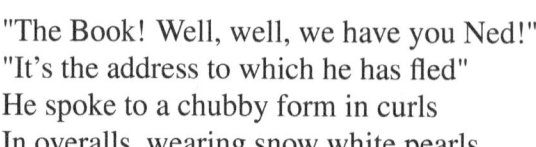

"The Book! Well, well, we have you Ned!"
"It's the address to which he has fled"
He spoke to a chubby form in curls
In overalls, wearing snow white pearls

"But this address! Its a message too!"
She exclaimed, "Which I must read to you"
"And I *will* explain, no worries there!"
"We must have given you quite a scare"

"Try Building One, by Things Castaway"
"Stop at Fairtokeep, by Camyer Way"
"Or Highway One will hurry one soon"
"To the City of Thieves, Salt Lagoon"

"Its an address, and a message too!"
"Its meant for us, and meant for you"
She paused, considered, then gave us
An explanation, that went thus:

A flower's happy on a plant
A leaf is happy on a branch
A pebble's happy on a beach
There is a loving home for each

Though many things may come your way
They aren't yours to take away
It's bad to take them as you roam
For it deprives them of their home

The reason isn't very deep
It isn't really fair to keep
Something that may just look foregone
Only because it's chanced upon

Quite often, things that come your way
Belong to someone in some way
They can be very dear sometimes
Be memories of precious times

There may be someone sad out there
Searching for them in much despair
Someone who pines for them, who may
Miss them so very much each day

Things that are taken really must
Be given, bought, asked for in trust
If cast away, they're fair to keep
Only if that makes no one weep

This strange lady in overalls
Had the soft look of worn-out dolls
With fuzzy hair, and twinkling eyes
She looked comforting, warm and nice

"I'm Dawn (I look like a cartoon)"
"Painter for the Magical Moon"
"Mr. Reed is here to help me find"
"My stolen colors, peace of mind"

"Oh! You can have mine!" rang Tommy's voice
"Please take all crayons of your choice"
"Why thank you Tommy, thanks indeed!"
"But... here's what I really need!"

No sooner had she said these words
We heard the calls of ocean birds
No starry skies, no longer night
It was a beach in broad daylight!

But something, really, wasn't right
Everything here was gray and white!
The sandy beach spread miles along
Colorless waves swished up a song

A quaint white cottage faced the beach
A boundary wall, within our reach
A wooden gate led through the wall
Low, and fringed with vines of fall

The vines, of colors, had no hints
Their leaves were white, they had no tints
Neither did, in that large compound
Trees, flowers, leaves, twigs on the ground

"I paint for the Magical Moon"
"I paint all – sea, sky or lagoon"
"I choose each hue and every shade"
"Of all things nature ever made"

"I paint all blossoms bright each day"
"The gold of wheat and fawn of hay"
"I paint bluebells blue, and lilies white"
"And I paint mist grey on the hillside"

"I pick the hues, I decide their range"
"Decide how exactly they will change"
"The sea that's blue-green in the day"
"At night I paint indigo-gray"

"But look around, what do you see?"
"My colors! Gone! Stolen from me!"
"How could they *steal* them? Why did they?"
"I'm so very disturbed today!"

The little coon looked very stressed
Guilty and very much distressed
Quite mystified, curious to know
I asked "Please, could you tell us more?"

Mr. Reed sported a pensive look
Like a sleuth in a mystery book
"I'm Detective Reed, How do you do?"
"Very delighted to meet you!"

He pointed to the vines on the wall
"A shame those have no colors at all"
"They were stolen by a chap who's fled"
"From celestial jail – his name is Ned"

"A petty thief: no scruples, strings"
"Lifts colors, tunes and sundry things"
"But he won't get far, I'm on his trail"
"I'll haul him back to celestial jail"

But what was that? By the cottage stood
My new car, with a note on its hood!!
"Destination:" it read "Two way run"
"To the City of Thieves, Highway One"

When I showed it to detective Reed
He exclaimed "Fantastic! Wow! Indeed!"
"I always use my official van"
"But I'll drive a mooncar, when I can!"

Our new adventure thus begun,
We sailed along on Highway one
The moonbeam car just seemed to glide
Through towns, villages and countryside

Soon we reached a hill, rather tall
With rolling slopes, and a waterfall
Just in front, in a delicate tie
Was a rainbow stolen from the sky

The clouds in the sky sported a frown
In a huff were searching up and down
As we passed by it, a gentle spray
Of a searching raincloud, blew our way

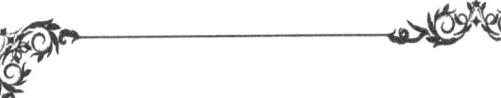

We passed a lagoon, and presently
Were where we had set out to be
A sign proclaimed, beneath the leaves
"Government Complex, City of Thieves"

A pretty city where nothing matched
Most things had been stolen and patched
Presently, a road sign said *"High Way"*
We drove along some miles that way

We came upon *"Inn Faretoukip"*
"For gourmet food and refreshing sleep"
We stopped and Reed went in to find
A map, just for his peace of mind

Consulting it, he drove around
And Things Castaway was quickly found
It was where the gray road made an arc
Around a beautiful central park

Here Reed left us, said he'd be back
As soon as Ned was found and nabbed
"The force is searching as we speak"
"This could be a nasty hide-and-seek"

The city streets were lined with flowers
Cottages, gardens, tall bell-towers
Roads stretched miles along the lagoon
Like a halo drawn around the moon

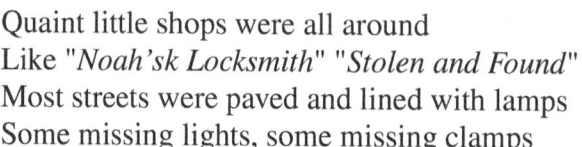

Quaint little shops were all around
Like "*Noah'sk Locksmith*" "*Stolen and Found*"
Most streets were paved and lined with lamps
Some missing lights, some missing clamps

Picket fences, buildings and homes
Gardens with figurines of gnomes
Many colorless trees and palms
On which dangled lush fruits, like charms

And some structures in sundry lanes
Had missing doors and missing panes
We walked around the park to see
Explore more of this strange city

A sign we saw said "*Alcazar*"
It led to a stolen goods bazaar
Within, what mayhem we did find!
It had stolen goods of every kind!

But in this funny place we saw
Its patrons had a serious flaw
They bought one, stole two, what a deal
Stole stolen goods for more appeal

How many steals were they removed
From one transaction, only proved
How highly placed would those be who
Stole from the thieves who stole from you

We wondered, pondered, stared at eaves
We counted birds, and counted leaves
Debated how the folks here chose
The Mayor of the City of Thieves

An old man came up, said hello
And told us things we didn't know
"The most wanted professions here"
"Are key-scraping and oversmear"

"There's a short supply of camouflage"
"Of colors and of paints at large"
"Aha! Now I see! Holy Saints!"
"So that's why Ned stole all my paints!"

"Its a business that's in great demand"
"Bring a red one in, poof! Turn it sand"
"You'd be filthy rich in just two days"
"Oversmearing – best business, always!"

"Got him!" It was Reed, full of cheer
"He was in fact very close to here"
"We found him when we launched a search"
"In Building One, it's behind that church"

"Like beacons up on floor thirteen"
"Most gaudy drapes that we had seen"
"Inside, from the bottom to the top"
"Were colors sploshed to his doorstop!"

"We unlocked the door with one of these"
Said Reed, showing us my car keys!
On one was stamped in bright colors
"M.M. Locksmiths and Farriers"

"Inside was Ned, with the stolen things"
"Paints, easels, brushes, other things"
"He was read his rights, ushered away"
"Right back to jail – he's on his way"

He gave the colors and the rest
To Dawn, who was thankful but distressed
"They're all so smeared! Oh what a waste!"
"To be splurged in such abhorrent taste"

We were back on her doorstep now
Dawn had a deep frown on her brow
"I think Ned even took my keys!"
"From under this mat! Help me please!"

From my pocket came a sudden clink
The special key! On my key link!
"Try this!" I handed her the bunch
"A magic key," I said on a hunch

Sure enough, it was a perfect fit
And we went it, Oh what a treat!
With palettes, colors now restored
Dawn's happy, sprightly spirit soared

With a wave she said "Let me show you!"
And brushed the sky indigo blue
Then lightly with a silky brush
She applied to it a peachy flush

With orange on the afternoon sky
It turned to dusk like a hiding spy!
We had so much fun with Dawn that day
As she painted everything our way

So the sky turned white, gold, then pink
Then blue, then violet in a blink
Her home, no longer white and black
Looked charming, with its colors back

Around it was the sandstone wall
Low and draped with vines of fall
Brown, rust, yellow, green and mint
Each leaf had a different tint

She took us through a shell-paved lane
To a town that looked odd and plain
But strange it was! With curious things
Like a raven with a swallow's wings

"His wings were stolen, so he wears"
"His swallow friend's, who gave her spares"
We saw galore, such things of lore
Until we could impose no more

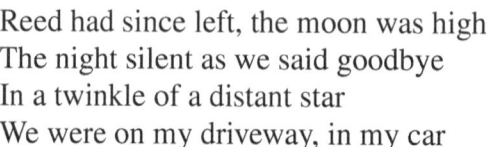

Reed had since left, the moon was high
The night silent as we said goodbye
In a twinkle of a distant star
We were on my driveway, in my car

A barn owl called, a crane flew by
Dropped a note in patterns of tie-dye
"Thank you!" It said, "Lovingly, Dawn"
She'd be back with the colors of morn

We trundled to the attic now
The curtains looked colored somehow
The coon's purposeful tap on the lyre
Made the pen send a celestial wire

To Jimmy, in words soft as fleece
"Sir, May I return your lyre, please"
"I'll never ever steal again"
"I'll always be honest as rain"

A gust of spray blew in, in tune
With a "Hah!," a "Bah!," a clouded moon
And in that gust of misty spray
The book of runes turned cloudy gray

On my window with sparkles of light
Stars appeared, some were faint, some bright
Some wayward, furtive, shining low
Brightened, shone with an honest glow

Then more of them, curious, swarmed
Listened to my answer, charmed
Then pulsing, chuckling, off they went
Laughing to their heart's content

The book of runes lay damp and gray
Like a sculpture made of moistened clay
Of an oracle who seemed to know
Which way the next mistral would blow

The stars were dancing in a row
The ninth one first, four more to go!
"Ask another, Tommy! Yes, please do!"
"Oh no," he said, "this one's for you!"

The Diplomat

QUESTION NINE, couldn't be missed
It was colored, flowy, had a twist
You might wonder how a question might
Have such designs in a form so trite

It happened on that starry night
As the ninth star flashed its vagrant light
There were facets to it, like a gem
One hundred ninety five of them

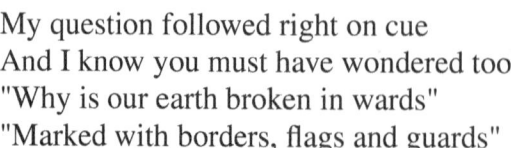

My question followed right on cue
And I know you must have wondered too
"Why is our earth broken in wards"
"Marked with borders, flags and guards"

"Though the sun and skies belong to none"
"Though the earth belongs to everyone"
The pen, stoically drew some signs
Like guards patrolling border lines

The lines perfectly straightened now
Displayed the words that just somehow
Looked more like armaments than runes
As gusts of wind blew anthem tunes

A strange display, some runes became
Poised armaments, while others, tame
They rippled in the gusts like rags
A hundred ninety five odd flags

To each anthem, some pages turned
On each, events restlessly churned
I saw crowds and homes, and factories
I saw newsprint over every crease

And on a sheet of iron, wrought
United stood some lines of thought
On this thoughtful sheet's gentle slope
That moonlit night, fell a ray of hope

"Please stand back, Sir!" I heard someone
A guard on a moonbeam, with a gun
On that tarry moon-road, long and wide
I saw him standing to one side

Imposing, tall and rather stern
He was not in fact the only one
I saw then marching from afar
More guards, around a shiny car

A dapper form emerged from it
Walked to the desk and took a seat
The book was given to him there
By his guards who handled him with care

Bewildered by this whole tableau
And this man who seemed important so
We waited, Tommy, coons and I
As he read the lines, his tone quite dry

"Ahem!" he said "Well, this does seem"
"A left wing trial balloon in theme"
"Well, we shall see," he said with poise
Read more lines in a dubious voice

"What happens (what's this?) goes on to state"
"Yard? Oh well, yard. What happens. Wait"'
"Hum. Div– Division. I don't agree!"
"Oh well, I'll read anyway, let's see"

"Strife? Strifes are (what?) fences from within"
"I don't agree, this is rather thin"
"For want of kindness, pure and true"
"Strifes and fear and (bah!) need ensue"

"Goodwill and trust then cast aside"
"Hum... build fences, walls and seek to hide"
"Nonsense!" he said, "This is isn't why"
"A hundred ninety five flags fly"

Of the many lines that glowed so clear
He mumbled most, which we couldn't hear
"Bah!" he said with a haughty look
"Let me explain, disregard this book"

"Who are you, Sir?" then Tommy said
He glowered, and turned tomato red
"I'm the Premier of the greatest land"
"That's in the Magical Moon's command"

"I am President Elect, surely you'd know"
"From Coyote News on Channel Four"
"Oh! Then," said Dad coon, "you must be"
"Mr. Archibald Bullwinkle Hucklebee"

A grin lit up Mr. Hucklebee's face
Looked pleased as punch, now full of grace
From charging to charming, in no time
He now spoke a dozen to a dime

Of the lines that we had barely heard
He differed with (just) about one third
A politic speech, designed to rouse
"I demand!" to a fictitious house

"That this be revised," he continued
A hushed, pronounced silence ensued
"I propose a bill to amend this book"
There were such loud thumps, the benches shook!

A bill he produced, in a trice
Then shouted "Filibuster!" twice
From then on he was quite irate
Engaged in an endless debate

We had't noticed, but now we all
Sat at the back of a senate hall!
From the podium, in command
He waved a bill of sorts in his hand

There really was no answer here
In his words, no message was clear
The answer was as hard to track
As needle in a senate haystack

Why did the moon have such a land?
To study perhaps, or understand...
I fell asleep, listening this man
'Til the session of questions began

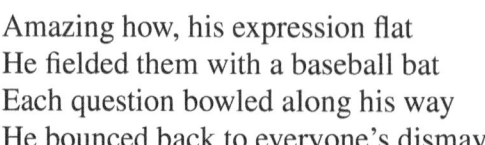

Amazing how, his expression flat
He fielded them with a baseball bat
Each question bowled along his way
He bounced back to everyone's dismay

His eloquent answers were a blur
No matter what the questions were
To each he answered this and that
Was a truly gifted diplomat!

We were drowsy, weary, circumspect
As the session ended, and he left
Fading in the light of the moon
With hot air, and an anthem tune

Like morning sunlight falls on snow
Starlight now glowed on my window
The stars were gathered, all to hear
The answer to the question, clear

I wondered then what I could say
I had no answer, yay or nay
Perhaps as far as I could tell
Flags wouldn't fly when all was well

But the answer really wasn't that
What I recalled from the bureaucrat
Was really meaningless, thus I
Said so to the stars that dallied by

They nodded, winked and seemed to say
"We know their whistle-stopping way"
"They go from word to word but still"
"They speak no answers, never will"

"In their speeches most articulate"
"Those words by scions of the state"
"Are sometimes clear, but often not"
"It all depends on quite a lot"

Tommy, I, and my friend, the coon
Gazed in thought at the magical moon
On his diplomatic haw and hum
Mr. Winkle made us ponder some

The stars dispersed, the attic quiet
The tenth question dispatched a light
Its beacon seemed to wax and wane
Clear as crystal, right as rain

Their Holiness

QUESTION TEN, of Tommy wore
A veil of fog, from the mystic shore
Of a sea of doctrines, tenets, norms
With restless waters, milling storms

So simply asked, without pretense
Some questions are just so intense
That an Augur who can answer these
Is a beacon over stormy seas

Like an elk on risky trails it walked
The pen walked lines that interlocked
As if they knew what words would come
The lines with worry, knotted some

"Why does Jill wear a cross, and Oulail..."
"Wear a white thobe, and Elma a veil?"
"Why is there a Kippah on Ed's head?"
"And a bindi on Minni's forehead?"

The pen, much like a sleeping bird
Or one in trance, didn't write a word
Tommy's gentle eyes brimmed with fear
"I've driven away the moon! Oh dear!"

But as a teardrop rolled and fell
The pen furiously wrote a spell
Like an archer, paused, focused and taut
Frees the swiftest arrow ever shot

The words were woven through the plots
Clung tightly to the tightest knots
The lines grew heavy, settled down
On them, runes built the strangest town

It had statues, temples, holy stalls
Monuments, buildings, domes and walls
Amid these, for pilgrims from afar
You'd see spires of a tall minar

Chants and prayers you could hear
Sermons, preachings, loud and clear
More and more were sung along
Until the chants became windsong

It deeply stirred the magic book
And for a short time, it did look
As its pages gently blew apart
That some spell had touched its heart

The spell then chose a page that was
The center of the book because
It gravely balanced weight and might
Its left was equal to its right

Then a veil of fog began to form
Outside my window, like a storm
It wafted in like holy smoke
And draped my attic like a cloak

In my attic, by the old doorway
Was a stand on which a soft quilt lay
A little sofa by its side
Just large enough for us to hide

We grabbed the quilt – my friends and I
Dove under it, drew it up high
In this makeshift tent, we sat still
Trembling so from the foggy chill

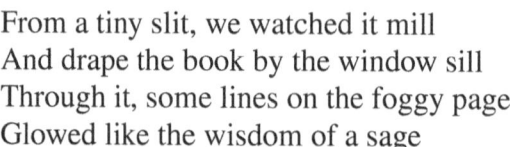

From a tiny slit, we watched it mill
And drape the book by the window sill
Through it, some lines on the foggy page
Glowed like the wisdom of a sage

Like a lantern shining through a wall
Of fog between two trees in fall
Like a wanderer, alone at night
Might feel when bathed in morning light

We were a little fearful then
Not knowing what would happen when
We waited, bated-breath, subdued
Oh what commotion then ensued!!

By the window, to our great surprise
We saw a crowd of the Old and Wise
Ministers, Deacons, Pundits, Priests
Elders of many many creeds

Senseis, Monks, Cantors, Oh my!
Dastoors and a Very Tall Rabbi
I counted thirty six at least
From the West and South and North and East

People in garbs of varied kinds
People who spoke aloud their minds
All at once, they talked above
Each other, jostled, lost no love

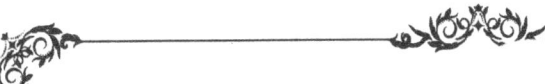

A tiny giggle, then a half
And then we couldn't help but laugh
Then Tommy, coons and even I
Laughed until it made us cry

For all at once they tried to read
The runes appealed to every creed
Some words we heard from one Imam
When a Swami yelled the name of Ram

"Shut up!" said a Roshi, "You're insane!"
A Manbo wonked him with a cane
They jostled shoved, and one let fly
Pulled the Rabbi's beard and punched his eye

"You Babalorisha! Get off that page!"
"Says who?" yelled the affronted sage
They fought and yelled, but then that rush
Suddenly quietened to a hush

"Help me!" From the window came a shout
My little friend had fallen out!
From the din, in fear, he'd bolted out
He clung to the ivy (just about)

The Swami conjured up a rope
A Manbo clambered down its slope
The Rabbi reached out, pulled them in
The coon huddled, all eyes on him

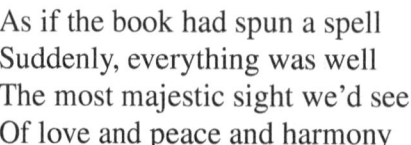

As if the book had spun a spell
Suddenly, everything was well
The most majestic sight we'd see
Of love and peace and harmony

From the book, they jointly read
The runes like beads strung on a thread
"Different trees have different seeds"
"Even grasses, weeds and river reeds"

"In different places, born apart"
"Each is of earth, an important part"
"Let me explain! Please!" came a voice
They all agreed – Yes, a good choice

This was a grave matter of fact
To be handled with the greatest tact
Each ignored what the other wore
No garb was less, as no leaf was more

From amidst them, in a leafy garb
Stepped up a Hounjan, thin and sharp
"It is as it is" said he, "No pun!"
"We wear what we wear, but we are one"

"We're born just so, its not our choice"
"We don't choose our bodies, or voice"
"And so we must not let all this"
"Business of garbs cause prejudice"

"A tree is a tree, a rose, a rose"
"When they're together, a forest grows"
"The greatest deeds are done when we"
"Live in peaceful, blissful harmony"

"What a lovely answer, and so wise!"
Tommy said, with admiring eyes
With reverence, for he was a gem
Threw back the quilt and bowed to them

So pleased were they, that one Munir
Who was a Yogi and Fakir
Invited us to his holy land
To cleanse our souls! He waved his hand

In an instant, on the count of three
We stood under a Banyan tree
It had the widest trunk, and around
Its branches swinging to the ground

It was a warm and sunny day
Sharp aromas came our way
The Banyan tree had the coolest shade
A thick canopy of green jade

An exotic place, and quiet too
We heard the call of a sole cuckoo
The swish of leaves, as branches swayed
In a grove of trees of light and shade

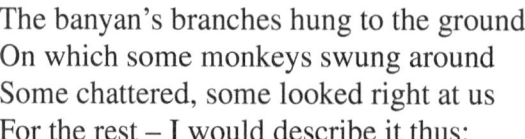

The banyan's branches hung to the ground
On which some monkeys swung around
Some chattered, some looked right at us
For the rest – I would describe it thus:

Around a Banyan trunk
On a wide bench of clay
Protected by its shade
Sat the yogi by the day

Always cross-legged he sat
In his summer wardrobe
A saffron and orange
Colored, wrapped cotton robe

On his forehead were lines
Drawn of sandalwood paste
There were three stripes across
Looking sagely and chaste

A 'U' drawn on each arm
And a dot within each
And a brass drinking pot
He had within arm's reach

With a bun on his head
Of his long matted hair
Which rested just below
His waist, on his chair

By his perch, sandals made
From wood of mango tree
And there, cross-legged he sat
With one hand on a knee

The other on a rest
Made of hand-hewn hard teak
Thus the yogi from dawn
Sat 'til dusk's orange streak

Around him there were trees
Many Cassias and Neem
And Mangoes and Drumsticks
Sun and shade in between

Just beside this yogi
Just a stone's throw away
Was a village enclave
With few homes made of clay

From early dawn to dusk
People bustled about
Most were calm and content
And were rather devout

Each morning through the year
People would bring him food
And other offerings
In clay pots, or of wood

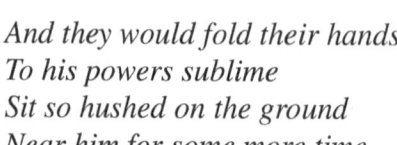

And they would fold their hands
To his powers sublime
Sit so hushed on the ground
Near him for some more time

Some would light up joss sticks
Planting them by his side
Their smoldering aroma
Would then spread far and wide

Jasmines and Patchouli
Sandalwood, myrrh and clay
The yogi's surroundings
Were the sweetest bouquet

Interlaced with the smell
Of the blossoms around
On summer afternoons
The yogi from his ground

Would preach and would mumble
Softly some holy chants
And speak words of wisdom
Off the seat of his pants

"Always lie with your feet"
"Pointing straight to the east"
"Sing a prayer at dawn"
"It keeps the Gods appeased"

On the Banyan, monkeys
Swung around and about
They'd often sit by him
Contemplating the crowd

Though the Yogi and they
Weren't really friends
They joined in his preachings
With profound verbal blends

Sometimes he'd also bless
A new cow, or a calf
Accept a banana
And then return one half

He had a little hut
In a lovely enclave
Surrounded by lush trees
Here he kept all they gave

There was a stream nearby
That danced along its way
Its crystal clear waters
Cool on a summer day

Often from the village
From across the mangroves
At dawn, noon and late dusk
Wafted smoke from clay stoves

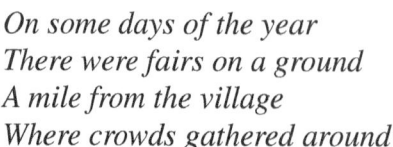

On some days of the year
There were fairs on a ground
A mile from the village
Where crowds gathered around

From neighboring villages
With some fields in between
All knew everyone here
Always a festive scene

In this idyllic world
There lay the deepest calm
A religion's true soul
And its profoundest charm

We didn't know we were back until
The attic sounds began to mill
Goodbyes were said through force of will
So sublime was this Yogi's skill

The fog dispersed, a cloud flew by
Pinpoints of stars dotted the sky
The book lay thin as a parchment now
Its pages gone, vanished somehow

The holy men then very soon
Went home to the Magical Moon
Each a ship, with a different sail
Doctrine, sect, theological trail

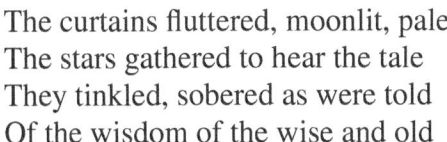

The curtains fluttered, moonlit, pale
The stars gathered to hear the tale
They tinkled, sobered as were told
Of the wisdom of the wise and old

It was rather quiet that night
The eleventh question shone its light
The prince of princes, king of kings
Its crown, the shiniest of things

Two people with us, strong and fair
Demanded nothing, always there
I wanted Dad coon, and Mom coon
To also share the magical moon

So thoughtful, more than I could say
They agreed to ask one each, that day
Dad coon said "Go ahead, dear Gwyn"
But Mom coon asked him to begin

The Pot of Gold

QUESTION ELEVEN was indeed
The king of want and prince of need
Had haunted all for centuries
Had ruled people's philosophies

Dad coon summed it up in his words
The flow of rivers, flight of birds
"Why," said he "do we all contend"
"To the pot of gold at the rainbow's end"

"Why, through wilderness are we bound"
"For the happiness that's never found"
The pen, dutiful as a clock
Etched chisel marks on lines like rock

Through a mountainside hewn freshly through
Through wet rocks, cut straight, or askew
The lines were roads that seemed to try
To reach the rainbow in the sky

The wind blew with a scent of hope
Of lilies on a grassy slope
Whistling through the mountains thus
It ruffled the Magnum Opus

The wind rattled the window pane
Brought a rumor of torrential rain
Around it, clouds began to swell
On the book a bolt of lighting fell

On the open page, it shattered lines
Like raw diamonds from diamond mines
As the thunderbolt smoldered away
There, jewels of their memories lay

Surely none could read these, of course
This pièce de résistance, tour de force
Dad coon was quiet, perhaps he knew
Who'd read the answer for him, too

A distant rumble from a cloud
Sounded like footsteps, growing loud
Somewhat afraid, we huddled by
The magic book, and heard a sigh

"A difficult question, I must say..."
Said someone from the moonlit doorway!
"Please do not be afraid of me"
"I'm Advisor of Philosophy"

A philosopher! Why, his presence
Retrospectively, did make sense!
With a grave expression, thoughtful look
He walked with purpose to the book

Both hands on the desk, in support
He studied quietly their import
The jeweled lines in his shadow
Grew brighter, clearer, even more

Then softly he began to read
Those lines that spoke a lot indeed
They told of journeys that unfold
Down mountain paths that lead to gold

Down seas and plains and meadows and
Through rains and ice and desert sand
"That's all," he said, with a final look
And closed the pages of the book

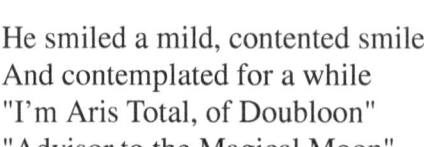

He smiled a mild, contented smile
And contemplated for a while
"I'm Aris Total, of Doubloon"
"Advisor to the Magical Moon"

Dad coon solemnly nodded then
As if he'd known from way back when
Aris explained then: "Happiness"
"Is not in things you can possess"

"Look up above, what do you see?"
"Beneath that rainbow, flying free"
"Happy birds, like a sailing ship"
"They ride the winds, soar high and dip"

How did this happen? So amazed
We looked around us, rather dazed
On a path, with mountains all around
We were in a coach, outward bound

No horse, no engines, nothing there
The coach just glided on thin air
With the path, it rounded every bend
Following it to the rainbow's end

We went, as morning turned to day
By mountains, meadows, fields of hay
We stopped in towns with funny names
And we played the funniest games

Many hours passed that day in fun
A beautiful ride for everyone
So smooth, that we almost forgot
We sought to reach a jeweled pot

Aris, with us, had all along
Hummed his own enchanted song
We didn't want the ride to end
As the path now turned its final bend

The rainbow shining high above
Dipped out of sight, behind a grove
Aris then pointed to the way
To where the pot of fortunes lay

But here we paused, more than a tad
The journey over, we were sad
We didn't want the jeweled pot
Aris then said "That's what I thought!"

"I wanted you to search your soul"
"Happiness isn't a distant goal"
"It's always in the here and now"
"In the rainbow *with* you high above"

"Its the journey, with your dearest friends"
"Not the pots of gold at rainbow-ends"
"Its my advice, and here I say"
"Carpe diem, friends, seize the day!"

The dusk had fallen, it was chill
A light winked on a distant hill
"Look! That's your home!" Tommy exclaimed
Like a cottage in a painting, framed

The sofa was the coach, in fact
The quilt around us, still intact
Aris, beside the book, now closed
Said "I must go, be happy folks!"

The stars then gathered all around
A happy answer we had found
The treasured tale of the rainbow ride
Is told by stars since, far and wide

The dozenth question, colored green
For Mom coon, really, should have been
But reaching out for the next draw
Mom coon was fast asleep, I saw

The smell of grass on the lily slope
The happy ride on the path of hope
And such memories, always to keep
Had cradled her to happy sleep

The Quack

QUESTION TWELVE a little faint
Was really a half-complaint
It bounced from Mom coon first to me
From me, then, it bounced to Tommy

Then it bounced to the little coon
Then back to Tommy, very soon
On the coon's behalf, we heard him say
"Why must we eat fruits and greens each day?"

The pen, as always quite precise
Italicized to emphasize
First, the *fruits* in "fruits and greens"
Then the *greens* in "fruits and greens"

The lines looked sleepy, quivered less
The pen wrote slowly, nonetheless
Lazily, with a doodle touch
Food did not excite them much

The pen then embellished the "and"
And left all words remaining, bland
No sooner had it written so
Runes on them began to grow

Sprouts appeared in patterns fine
In many lines after each line
Like furrows with produce and yield
That are planted in a farmers field

They grew into the truest greens
Peas and broccoli, lettuce, beans
Beside them an orchard took root
Laden with nuts and luscious fruit

A zephyr brought the sound of flutes
From lands of druids and carnutes
From celtic fields, it blew right in
Singing about the Loire and Seine

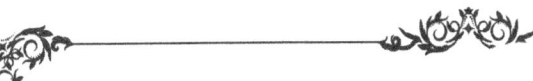

The crinkle of the pages when
The magic pages turned again
Composed a very celtic tune
Crooned an ode to the magical moon

The symphony that played along
The well-composed enchanted song
Was squired by the gleam of stars
And by the rustling of the grass

The pages, searching for the soul
Of the music, seemed to find their goal
They settled on two pages wide
As the searching moonrays fell inside

On the settled pages, just a line
Glistened like jade in bright sunshine
The answer, short, unlike before
Seemed somewhat less, and not much more

When bang! – a thump, a crashing sound!
"Hey!" Startled, we looked all around...
"Your l- license please, and insurance!"
A yell, a grumble, then suspense

"I wonder where the b- bloke has gone"
"A h- hit and run, if ever one!"
"Looney, with a b- bird in his beard!"
"I wonder where he d- disappeared!"

This character looked quite confused
We stood there watching him, amused
A concussion? But it was not
He seemed to be a mild crackpot

A vine of grapes around his neck
His corded sandals, now a wreck
Dressed in a linen robe, absurd
On his wide-brimmed hat, perched a bird

A macaw with the wings of quail
A pheasant's crest and a magpie's tail
In great comfort the creature sat
Of hats, this was the strangest hat

No sooner had he read the line
The bird let out a shriek feline
"You're right my dear, this is too terse"
He read again, this time in verse

"A hundred eighteen needed by"
"Creatures that swim or walk or fly"
"These elements are all around!"
"In fruits and greens they can be found"

He seemed to relish what he'd read
In great enjoyment, then he said
"Greetings to you, I'm Barden Flutes"
"Physician to the brave Carnutes"

"Sometimes I volunteer to be"
"A dietician, so the moon called me"
"I'm a doctor of a different kind"
"With my formulae I heal the mind"

With most systems he didn't agree
Had an M.D.O.D.G. degree
After a B.S.E.T.C.
And from Autricum, a Ph.D.

"A hundred eighteen elements make"
"*Every*thing, be it fruit or fruitcake"
"To be sharp, we need a healthy mind"
"Need elements of a certain kind"

"Your intellectual powers to-date"
"Completely stem from what you ate"
"If you just ate crab apples each day"
"You'd grow pincers and scuttle away"

"My science, noted by my colleagues"
"Is discussed in the medical leagues"
"The greatest studies on my theme"
"Are by my colleague, Neem Hakim"

"If you ate certain rare proteins"
"Such as those found in blue-green beans"
"You could (just like this) wave your hand"
"And a genie from a distant land..."

"Would then appear and then you could"
"With supplemental peas you should"
"Bid that he (or her) conjure for you"
"A castle, cottage or igloo"

There was a pause, then a hurricane
We heard a "Hah! Its you again!"
"Butternut Flutes of Kwajalein!"
"Did you now forget your sugarcane?"

"And what about your walnut diet?"
"Can you not wave from left to right?"
We heard much grumbling, then a tweet
We were in a field of cane and wheat!

There stood a cottage, made of oak
Right by a pond with frogs a-croak
And beside it, in his dressing gown
Stood Aflatoon! with a scowl and frown

The strange physician of Carnutes
The one and only Doctor Flutes
Stood perplexed, and scratched his beard
At why all of this had appeared

He also didn't quite respond
To Aflatoon, beside the pond
Across it, grew a nut forest
At which he gazed, with interest

Now where was I? said Doctor Flutes
On the subject of blue-green fruits. . .
Then "Pul-chri-tud-inous!" we heard
That couldn't be a Mynah bird!

A sonorous voice said "Now let's see!"
"A telegram, addressed to me"
"To hold a class for a *B. Flutes*"
"On the subject of nuts and dry fruits"

Flutes just gaped, did not answer
This Agronomic Professor
"I suggest we go to Section three"
"Where now we have a classroom free"

And so for some time, we were free
To roam the countryside and see
The wonderful fields, the forestry
With Aflatoon, the dear Genie

Delighted to see Aflatoon
We walked with him that afternoon
He wore today his dressing gown
Apologized for dressing down

"He's not supposed to wave his hand"
"It's an *instant* summon, a command"
"And though he preaches fruits and beans"
"Often forgets his nuts and greens"

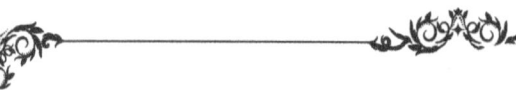
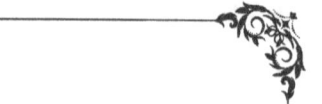

"From springtime, not counting today"
"I've been summoned eleven times this way"
"But on a magical moon, I'm free"
"To prescribe for him a remedy"

It all made sense now, after all
Genies must always be on call
A powerful Djinn, a jolly one
However, he said this wasn't fun

"But then what could poor Siebel do?"
"Ho ho!," he boomed, "Let me show you!"
"But we must not let Siebel know"
"I'll take you there incognito"

He led us through the cottage door
A classroom! We'd been here before!
There were other students too within
And Siebel, ready to begin

Aflatoon, the powerful Djinn
Made us vanish as we filed in
On a back-bench there he sat with us
For the exec-ed on edible nuts:

NUTS *he wrote with an underline*
His expression neutral and benign
And just to make a point more fine
Below it, he drew a second line

In reference to dietary needs
There are four <u>kinds</u> of nuts (or seeds)
From his pocket, he drew in his flow
Four nuts, and placed them in a row

<u>True nuts</u> are hard-shelled: true dry fruits
<u>Drupes</u> are nuts in seeds in fruits
Those in pods are <u>Angiosperm</u>
Ones with no enclosure: <u>Gymnosperm</u>

Respective examples: This Hazelnut
This Almond, Peanut, and Pine nut
Then he explained in great detail
What "Culinary Nuts" entail

"That's fine!" Exclaimed Doctor Flutes
"But in our forest of Carnutes"
"We have seventeen categories!"
"Based on their magic qualities"

"Hm," said Siebel, quite softly
"I see your point, and also see"
"That in your land of the brave and free"
"All nuts may not grow on a tree"

To the class he said, this time loudly
"Seventeen divisions there may be"
"But in my class, as we progress"
"We will have just four, nonetheless"

He began with the full inventory
Of True Nuts, with considerable glee
"Of the common ones, we have Acorn"
<"Poisonous!"> retorted Flutes, with scorn

Next we shall discuss Fagus
Known as Beech to all of us
Its a genus of deciduous trees
<"Its useless! Not enough Manganese!">

Unfazed, our scholar continued
In strict sequence, he then reviewed
The family of Fagaceae
Beginning from Fagus hayatae

He described Fagus sylvatica
Drew leaves of Longipetiolata
Explained life-cycles and the rest
Of an entire beech–maple forest

He spoke of Grandifolia's fruits
Amid remarks by Doctor Flutes
He addressed Fagus crenata
Then spoke of Fagus lucida

Continued with beech, on and on
How Asplenifolia, colored fawn
Grew on graceful trees, very tall
That turned a golden brown in fall

Then he expounded Hazelnut
Then Breadnut, and then Candlenut
As he went from Chestnut to Filbert
My inner ear began to hurt

Then in a swift, surprising stroke
In this class, pandemonium broke
Like a bull, with a broken yoke
Flutes charged up in a ball of smoke

Siebel dodged out of his path
Let the blackboard take his wrath
Flutes now flexed his Ph.D.
In this celestial university

He drew a star with seventeen
Clear prongs atop a deep tureen
Then he labeled them, all in green
From Diamine to Carotene

He didn't know, our Doctor Flutes
Famed physician of Carnutes
That in a magical classroom
A board's like a wand, or witch's broom

The ones in this university
Were as powerful as wands could be
With the slightest wave of his hand
The board would clean itself, turn bland

He gave up in a little while
Grumbling in therapeutic style
It was clear that he didn't agree
With principles of Agronomy

Siebel then waited until when
He went back to his seat again
Then he resumed, nonchalantly
With the Drupe – Canarium harveyi

. . .

That's all we heard, for Aflatoon
Got summons from the Magical Moon
He waved his finger, in a flick
We were back again in my attic!

"Couldn't he leave the class?" I asked
Aflatoon's joy was barely masked
"Oh no! You cannot leave too soon"
"No Sir, not on a magical moon!"

After that he fondly bid adieu
We waited, didn't know what to do
I must have dozed, for soon I woke
To thumps and squawks, was this a joke?

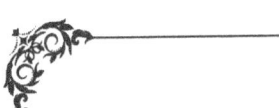

After what seemed an hour or two
Flutes was back to continue!!
In a huff, his face like Chilean peach
"Nuts shouldn't be allowed to teach!"

He launched into a public mass
Of what he thought of Siebel's class
Though a subtle fact did remain
He didn't wave his hand again!

There on my attic rug we lay
Listened to what he had to say
"I can cure any odd disease"
"My services are free of fees"

He then resumed his speech on greens
Interspersed with the hat-bird's memes
Who often squawked in agreement
Or flicked its beak in strong dissent

In his authoritarian way:
"If you eat an orange every day"
"Beginning from new moon, you may"
"Excel at music and ballet"

"Of the hundred eighteen elements"
"Gallium has greatest importance"
"It'll make you rich, give you potin"
"Its usually found in green protein"

"With Swiss chard and capsicum juice"
"No mathematics would confuse"
"Eat grapefruit with vermilion grapes"
"For all sorts of powers over shapes"

"On a solstice, though," said the sage
"Greens cause collateral damage"
"On that day you must eat three fruits"
"Of trees with yellow or pink shoots"

The answer seemed to be so deep
That everyone fell fast asleep
In the book of runes, that one sentence
Was quite long, in a dietary sense

Flutes, of course, was wide awake
He spoke for hours, give or take
Finally spent, like a candlestick
He waved goodbye, left my attic

Curious stars gathered around
By the window for the answer found
But here I was, could not recall
Hadn't had my Boggle nuts at all

I sounded mixed up, I confess
A voice yelled "Eat your watercress!"
A distant hoot, a flap of wings
A "Quack!" that said preposterous things

The little coon was full of awe
Wanted Powers, and a Great Macaw
He'd surely have, among others
Greens, nuts, and fruits of all colors

I thought the night had flown away
Surely the answer took all day
But here I heard a soft tick tock
Past the hour (barely) by the clock!

The final question, we would find
Was the highest-flying of its kind
Which Tommy, in a gentle voice
Asked sounding curious, but wise

The Merchant of the Bedouin

THE THIRTEENTH question was the last
Though the night was barely past
"Why," he said, "do tell me why"
"Raindrops fall, though eagles fly!"

No sooner had the pen finished
A thunderstorm appeared unleashed
Runes like clouds and falling rain
Appeared over rolling terrain

The lines were damp like gleaming roads
Dusk eagles flew to their abodes
Sprinkles of runes, like drizzling rain
Blew forward, upward, down again

A gust of spray came whistling in
A rattle on the roof, of tin
The pages blew off in a swarm
Like parchments in a prairie storm

Over the plains I saw them go
Meanwhile a single one, aglow
Still clinging to the binding, cast
The answer to the question asked

A tapping sound, at first discreet
Then turned to patter of four feet
Then the padding of almost a fleet
Of camels walking on concrete

"Outside the window!" came a shout
We rushed to it, and leaned far out
Outside, under the starry sky
Were a hundred camels walking by

"They're camels of a magic clan"
We looked back startled, at a man
With a brilliant smile, a coffee tan
"We bring treasures from Azerbaijan"

He looked gaunt, was tall and thin
Wore a thobe of dazzling white muslin
He crossed his arms, said with a grin
"I'm a merchant of the Bedouin"

"This book," he said, "I've seen before"
"In the mirrored palace of Tanjore"
"This book is legend for its lore"
"In a land I've traveled shore to shore"

"I see its torn, thinned to the bone"
"I see its pages have now flown"
"Once it's read, and the answer's known"
"It'll fly away to its magic throne"

There was something in the way he spoke
Like camphor scent in holy smoke
Like memories foggy days evoke
Like joss sticks made of mystic oak

A magic spell was all around
I shook my head, to shake it down
It was wicked wavered, swirled around
But your senses had to stand their ground

It cleared as he began to read
Slowly at first, then gathered speed
"For every person, plant or weed"
"It all begins with a fallen seed"

"It soars upward, and falls again"
"With weight of worry, chilling rain"
"Its a question of what has indeed"
"Greater command and greater need"

"For dominion is in everyone"
"Light is brighter than the sun"
"The bird can rise above the reed"
"By flapping wings of mindful deed"

The spell was back, or did it seem
That the lines had lost their gleam
The page was fading from our view
A rolling storm began to brew

Abruptly, then he closed the book
"That's all..." he said with a puzzled look
"I've crossed these winds, in a land I roam"
"They've come to blow these pages home"

"We *must* leave quickly, hurry now"
"To my caravan, escape somehow"
"They bring great danger as they swell"
"At the end of every magic spell"

By the window, camels lined their back
On each a soft cotton-filled sack
Swiftly, we mounted, rode away
My car was also towed away

So began a journey through the sands
Through strange wonderful magic lands
The merchant's camels, in a row
With Toby's magic car in tow

As went by the sands of Mizar
We saw an oasis from afar
There, beneath the twinkling stars
Stood a lovely palace with minars

By a mystic lake it stood that night
White as snow in the starry light
Draped with bougainvilleas
Lined with roses and azaleas

The merchant pointed from afar
Said "Do you see that tall minar?"
There lives my dear friend, Aflatoon
He's area assistant to the Magical Moon

It was fun to ride the camels so
They were called by proper names and more
"Walk softly," he would tell Salim
"It's no time to snort!" He'd tell Wasim

"Don't gurgle, chomp at the dinner camp"
"It's not good manners, now Diramp!"
There was Selma, and a Loriyal
The one that towed was just called Sal

Some distance from the town Mizar
We stopped for the merchant's next bazaar
At a quaint place called "Holy Days Inn"
Run by a local landlord and Djinn

The next morning, we woke afresh
Had Manakish and warm Goulesh
Excited, then we stepped outside
To a magical vista, opened wide!!

In a burst of golden warm sunshine
In myriad shades of sepia wine
Stood a mystic town, and we just knew
It was enchanted through and through

Sunshine was cut in silky strands
In gossamer ribbons and bands
It bounced off railings, window panes
And paved its pathways, roads and lanes

The town had magic undertones
Its walls were built of mirror-stones
Though fleetingly they seemed of brick
That played a smoke-and-mirrors trick

Squinting, we walked, though not too far
Into the tents of a great bazaar
Inside we saw, to our surprise
The *most* unusual merchandise

"It's the great bazaar of Syritin"
Said the merchant of the Bedouin
"It trades in goods from everywhere"
"From prickly pear to silverware"

"Though every thing you buy or sell"
"In this bazaar, has a magic spell"
We followed him through it all day
A magic flea market, you'd say!

There he sold (and bought) exotic goods
Like tree-bark from celestial woods
He'd bind them with a few commands
Into books you could hold in you hands

Each book, like feather, smokey gray
If dropped, flapped pages, flew away
He had pens of reeds in brown and pink
"They can read your mind, write what you think"

"I once bought one from Altazar's land"
"That wrote on its own in perfect hand"
The coon, embarrassed, looked away
"I just borrowed it," I heard him say

As evening fell, all bought and sold
With his profits neatly stowed in gold
As our caravan moved on again
He began patiently to explain

"The earth attracts, and so all"
"Things fall to it, large or small"
"It has powers of the wizard kings"
"Like the sun, and all celestial things"

"Things rise and fall, win or lose"
"Spin or slide, it depends on whose"
"Powers increase now, from before"
"How they balance, less or more"

"Two things: will and thought today"
"From celestial laws can break away"
"Raindrops fall, but eagles fly"
"Its easy to see, really, why"

"With the powers of thought and deed"
"If you wished so, you could indeed"
"Ignore the earth, soar to the sky"
"Just like an eagle, rise and fly"

"If you didn't try to stay with all"
"If you stayed divided, you'd be small"
"You'd have less power, lesser worth"
"Like raindrops you would fall to earth"

"With this explained I leave, my friends"
"The storm's now spent, this magic ends"
"We'll meet again (and we will soon)"
"In your attic on a magical moon"

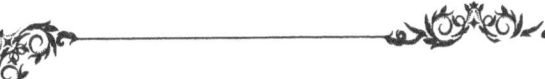

"This magic car will take you there"
"It was the one I bought in Éire"
"I sold it on the Moonbeam Isle"
"To a salesman... it has been a while"

"So I don't quite recall his name"
"He was a banker too, all the same"
"I gave him six keys by mistake"
"One of a door that I sold in Hague"

The merchant waved then, with a sigh
The camels tapped a soft goodbye
And so it left for magic lands
That caravan, over shifting sands

The sandy vista seemed to shift
To fawn and green, with clouds adrift
At first a few clouds, cotton white
Then dark and gray ones, like the night

With the thunder clouds, a falling rain
Formed over rolling terrain
Sprinkles of the drizzling rain
Blew forward, upward, down again

The roads were damp and wove around
On the lines of runes, we were homebound
As eagles flew to their abode
We saw a person by the road

Our magic car stopped in the rain
We asked him in, were off again
A gardener, going home from Meads,
He spoke of flowers, lawns and weeds

A cheerful man, wanted to know
How we were here, we told him so
Tommy described it rather fast
And then he, looking puzzled, asked

"In a muslin robe? Was his name Turin?"
"A merchant? Was he tall and thin?"
"He's a legend in this land you're in!"
"He's the Wizard of the Bedouin!"

We felt a spray and suddenly
We passed under the strangest tree
It had the widest canopy
With soft white branches, swinging free

Swaying gently all around
A Celestia that reached the ground
Falling droplets seemed to douse
A million diamonds on its boughs

We dropped him by a garden gate
He thanked us, mumbled he was late
It was a house that I had known
Of seven gables, made of stone

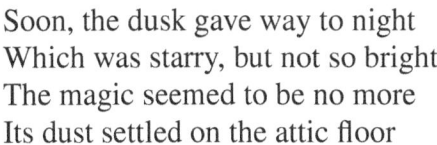

Soon, the dusk gave way to night
Which was starry, but not so bright
The magic seemed to be no more
Its dust settled on the attic floor

The attic's quiet, some stars I see
Seem to know the answers already
The coon's asleep, and Tommy too
The magical moon bids you adieu

The end

Magical Moon

The Harbingers

THAT YEAR, after the summer dust
Had cleared and leaves turned orange rust
The days were clear like crystalware
There was a faint chill in the air

The autumn crops were in the barn
In fields lay bales of golden yarn
Dry leaves were scattered on the ground
Some pumpkin patches grew around

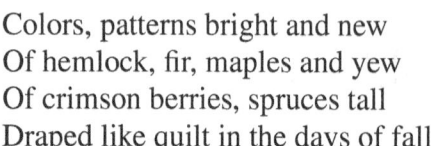

Colors, patterns bright and new
Of hemlock, fir, maples and yew
Of crimson berries, spruces tall
Draped like quilt in the days of fall

The autumn fair sold ears of wheat
Scarecrows, corn and apple treat
On porches, you'd see propped with ropes
Pumpkins, witches and autumn tropes

There was something in the air that day
Something strange to come my way
I saw it in so many ways
This day was not like other days!

The morning fog was gray, intense
I'd never seen one quite so dense
As if a cloud that couldn't fly
Had fallen from the stormy sky

The rumble of a thundercloud
Grew faint and loud and faint and loud
Like drumrolls from a distant land
Like the music of a marching band

From my window then I saw, agog
Marching soldiers, made of fog!
As this massive army sauntered by
The fog dispersed, the sun climbed high

I was puzzled and somewhat afraid
As the sunshine soon began to fade
A gust brought in a spray somehow
Though the sky was cloudless now!

What could this be all about?
Surely not... I began to doubt
Right then a robin said: "Phooey!"
Perched on a twig on the maple tree

That's what it said to everything
"Phooey!" it would always sing
But now there rang out in its trail
The softest croon of a nightingale!

To this, like jewels from a crown
Rain from the clear sky clattered down
The drops shone in the autumn light
A hail of diamonds, dazzling, bright

They blew like strands of beads, archaic
In a criss-cross harlequin mosaic
There was a strangely musical strain
To the pitter patter of this rain

A nightingale, a strange refrain...
This was surely that autumn rain
That could.. I thought, to my delight
That *would* herald *the* magical night!

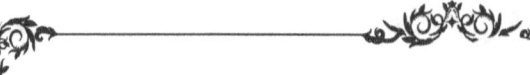

Like a horse galloping on a track
I flew upstairs, to my almanac
It said the moon was full tonight!
I skipped and danced in such delight!

What must I do? Where would I begin?
What if it were not... what if... what then?
Would there be...? I began to look
But saw no sign of the magic book

A noise outside, I thought I heard
Perhaps a trill of a mynah bird?
Perhaps..? Was it my friend, the coon?
But.. nothing there that afternoon!

I didn't know what was in store
I called my friends as the evening wore
Tommy, Mira, Leo, Salim
My closest friends, a wonderful team

Quite soon, the blue sky turned to pink
From peach to crimson, then to ink
The rain had stopped, a breeze blew by
Dry leaves rustled and then took flight

On the rug that lay on my attic floor
On the rocking chair beside the door
We sat, lay, kneeled, and waited there
Breathlessly, for the the night's affair

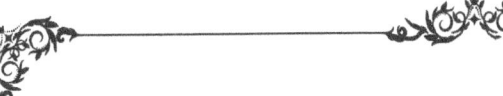

The inky sky was strange that night
Not a single star, nor cloud in sight
No sounds: not a whiff, a single cheep
The world seemed to have gone to sleep

And still, there simmered in the air
A lure you couldn't quite compare
To any feeling, thing or thought
To any dream, or story plot

So we waited, silent, didn't talk
Like a water-watching pelican flock
The night was silent, still as death
The winds waited with bated breath

With an hour past, I sauntered back
To my desk to look at the almanac
Was this the right year, day and page?
Right aeon, century and age...?

The alamanac, of course, was new
For just this year, through and through
Sure enough, there it was again:
"A full moon after harvest rain"

But the print beneath I hadn't seen!
It was *tiny*, read "Thirteen Fifteen"
"AM" it read, but it couldn't be so
Thirteen is a "PM", don't we know?

Then my friend Salim walked up to me
Leaned over, peered, so he could see
"That," he said, "does not make sense!"
"Unless..., I think we need a lens!"

But through the lens it read the same:
"Thirteen:Fifteen," and then, "AM"!
"Oh well!" I sat back on the rug
Gave the lens to Mira, with a shrug

As she waited, toying with the lens
She halted, gasped, and grew quite tense
"The clock! The clock! It's Thirteen Oh Nine!"
But the wall-clock showed Ten Fifty Nine!

"Let me look please!" Said Leo now
With a thoughtful wrinkle his brow
Tommy, quiet through all of this
Said, "Mira, can we look now, please?"

In a sequence now, our Pelican team
Looked through, then gasped, then gave a scream
Like the dancing fingers, in sequence
Of musicians, play their instruments

Like lyre birds in rehearsed concert
Each song was copied from the first
"Thirteen ten now!," then "thirteen eleven!"
"Now thirteen twelve!," "Oh God in heaven!"

I said those last words, as I gazed
Through the magnifying lens, amazed
The clock now showed thirteen bright stars
Like a constellation made of hours!

"Two minutes left!" I counted down
When Tommy nudged me, with a frown
"That's not the clock!" he said, for I
Had turned the lens towards the sky!

A bit confused, and somewhat vexed
I looked without the lens, perplexed
I thought I saw pinpoints of light
Thirteen stars in a circle tight!

Speechless, then I just pointed nigh
Through the attic window at the sky
As clouds drew apart, lo and behold
And magic tumbled from their fold!

Streaks of silvery rain criss-crossed
With streaks of starlight that were tossed
All over, bouncing off the seams
Of streaks of magical moonbeams

Did I dream? For I heard a "Geez!"
A faint stutter: "L- License please!"
"Did you hear that?" Leo shook his head
"Just fireworks perhaps," he said

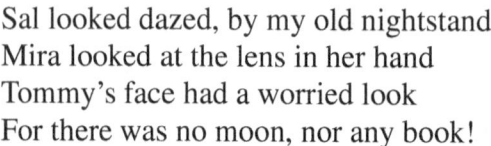

Sal looked dazed, by my old nightstand
Mira looked at the lens in her hand
Tommy's face had a worried look
For there was no moon, nor any book!

The Postman

QUI DOLOREM Ipsum Qia Dolor
There was a loud knock at the door
"Postman!" honked a nasal voice
Tommy leapt to the door in a trice

There he stood, with a bag of mail
A staunch racoon on his trail
In a night-blue uniform, no less
And a cap that read "M.M.P.S."

He gave me a parcel, wafer thin
Wrapped in a parchment, like glassine
With Lipsum words in brown and gold
And a postage stamp, large and bold

T'was gray like fog, and showed a grand
Big army, marching to a band
With neither address, nor postmark
And no instructions, no remark

No other writings I could see
No address and no addressee
Puzzled, I thought, what could it be?
"Sir, is this really meant for me?"

He nodded, said the strangest thing:
"Its special, like all mail I bring"
And then he gave a smart salute
Left, with the coon in hot pursuit

As we chatted keenly, something fell
"..away!" we heard, and then "...scoundrel!"
The coon came sliding on the floor
Right in, as the postman shut the door!

Then in pell-mell happened everything
As Tommy pulled at the parcel string
Look! Sal shouted, pointing high
To the moon that floated in the sky

An orb in milky luminous sheen
The largest I had ever seen
Filled my window, full and wide
Floating close by, just outside

Just as we realized that those
Stars and the moon weren't so close
"The parcel!" I heard Tommy scream
It had vanished as if in a dream!

"Look, look!" said Mira, pointing now
At the desk, that seemed to glow somehow
Like a lighthouse on a cliff, up high
Like the hearthrob of a firefly

On it, a book lay wafer thin
Though a million pages lay within
"It must be the book you spoke about!"
Leo exclaimed, then, with a shout

Tommy nodded, appeared solemn
Like the prophet of Jerusalem
He said, his tone quite circumspect
"Its the book of runes" with great respect

"Can we open it? And look inside?"
Sal eagerly stepped to its side
As I said "No..." we heard a din
And a shrill voice, angry, high and thin

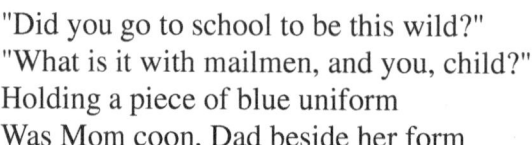

"Did you go to school to be this wild?"
"What is it with mailmen, and you, child?"
Holding a piece of blue uniform
Was Mom coon, Dad beside her form

Suddenly we heard from Sal a cry
A yelp of pain, than a gasp "oh my!"
Eyes surprised, his arm in a twist
Looking as if he had hurt his wrist

"This book" he gasped, "is hard as stone"
He clutched his wrist and gave a moan
"Oh no, Sal, do not pry it, please!"
It just opens to a magical breeze

"A *breeze*?" No gale could open this!
"No, Sal, let me explain this, please"
"I think I know how we must begin – "
"With the paper that it was wrapped in!"

We looked around, looked everywhere
But the parchment wrapper wasn't there
So strange! Wherever could it be?
Who unwrapped the parcel, did we see?

"Come out right now!" Mom coon was stern
"Hiding in there! When will you learn?"
The coon crept out from beneath the rug
Pulling at the wrapper, with a tug

And there he was, in the moonlight! Why!
Our friend, the little coon! Oh my!
But there was no time for friendly chat
No time for a hug, hello, or pat

The wrapper glinted, showed a hint
Of lines below each Lipsum print
"This parchment.." I began to say
When the print on it faded away

The lines now free, began to swing
Like gusts of wind blow skeins of string
"Leo, could you please hand me that..."
"White pen that lies beside your hat?"

Qui Dolorem Ipsum Qia Dolor
With it I wrote, as I did before
Qui Dolorem Ipsum Qia Dolor
I scratched that out, and wrote some more

But my words bounced off, rather stiff
Like pebbles rolling down a cliff
Mira then gave it a try
Then Sal, Leo, Tommy and I

"You see?" said I, "You must hold the pen"
"Steadfast, for the magic to begin"
"So steady – every word must stay"
"On a line, or it will fly away"

"Your question must be written so"
"Each word sits on a line, just so"
"It must not waver, must not bend"
"Perfectly cling from the start to end"

"And then you'll see your question turn"
"Into runes that glimmer, glow or burn"
"Or rain, or patterns of some frieze"
"To be whispered by the magic breeze"

"The breeze will blow over the runes"
"And chant them in enchanted tunes"
"The song will make the magic churn"
"You'll see a million pages turn"

"On the one on which your answer lies"
"The book will open, sage and wise"
Till a moonbeam shines in, milky white
And frames the answer in its light

"But then," I paused and looked at all
"You would be up against a wall"
"For the answer to your question would"
"Be in runes that can't be understood"

Crestfallen, Mira then said "Oh!"
"Then how, possibly, would we know?"
"The answer, then, what good is that?"
"Runes, chants, or magical pit-pat?"

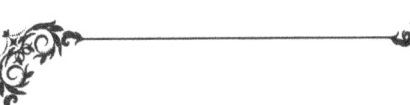

"You'll know!" Said Tommy with a grin
Giving them a mysterious spin
"Just wait and watch, that's my advice"
"It'll be a wonderful surprise!"

Leonardo, always thoughtful, wise
Said quietly, "Here is my surmise"
"If we can't write on these lines, well then"
"We must clearly find a magical pen!"

"Oh not again!" Mom's shriek rang out
The coon now held a pen in snout
"Where did you find that? This is bad!"
In a reprimanding voice, said Dad

To which the coon, before you know
Dropped it, and scurried out the door!
While all of us looked on, amused
"Oooh!" we turned back, now confused

"*Vel eum iure reprehenderit*"
It wrote on the lines "*..voluptate velit*"
The words, like ivy on a wall
Perfectly clinging to them all

And that night, with this magic pen
The magical moon was back again!
Like a stage conductor, to the roll
I turned around, and took control

"Look up, everyone, reach for the stars"
"There's one for each question of ours"
"They're precious, so pick just a few"
"Those that are meaningful to you"

"Do remember that your question must"
"Be honest, never break a trust"
"It must not be selfish, must not pry"
"It must not ever begin with *"I"*"

In my attic on the window sill
The curtain flapped, the night was still
A question in my mind took flight
A distant star burst into light

I reached for it, lo and behold
It was cold as crystal, hard to hold
It slipped out of my hand then, though
Became the first in a dancing row

Soon Sal and Mira picked one each
But Leo's question dodged his reach
But very soon he caught it so
It joined as fourth in line, aglow

Mom and dad and the little coon
Gazed in awe at the magic moon
When Tommy said "please do pick yours"
They just picked out three little stars

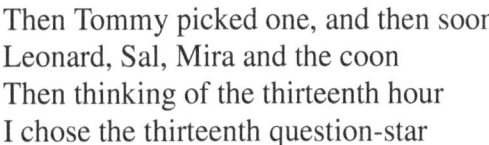

Then Tommy picked one, and then soon
Leonard, Sal, Mira and the coon
Then thinking of the thirteenth hour
I chose the thirteenth question-star

They danced in circles, and in flocks
Like a merry posse of peacocks
Some formed clusters, some formed blocks
Like the lovely blooms of hollyhocks

A soft tick tock filled up the room
Like fragrance of carnation bloom
The clock's hands ticked and tocked away
"It's question time," they seemed to say

The Augur

A SILENCE fell, you'd hear a pin
If it dropped on a wad of fine muslin
Not a breath, not a stir, all eyes on me
It was time for a question, finally!

With ragged breath, barely controlled
In a shaky voice, tepid then bold
I said, "Perhaps if we could all"
"Just look into a crystal ball.."

"And know what we will be one day"
"What we will do, what we will say"
"What kind of life will we peruse"
"What we will have, what we will lose"

"I think we'd then be all prepared"
"Would neither worry nor be scared"
"Can we see what the future holds?
"See what's ahead as time unfolds?

"Oh no no!" Came an urgent cry
"You didn't start it with a 'Why'!!"
It was Tommy, whispering, upset
"A why, a *why*,' did you forget?"'

"Of course! Oh no! how dense of me"
My heart sank almost instantly
I'd been so nervous, and so tense
That I had lost my better sense!

Now I wondered if perhaps I might
Perhaps.. perhaps just make it right?
Would the magic spell still remain
If I asked my question once again?

I cleared my throat, hesitantly
Chose my words quite carefully
Began to say "Why do we not.."
"I know it's here, the Bouncing Blot"

"Huh?" I wheeled around in a trice
That, of course, was not my voice!
Everyone turned back, startled so
Whirled back on hearing "I know!"

There! on the window sill! Said Sal
Propped on it was a crystal ball!
Inside was an attic just like mine
With a window, bathed in bright moonshine

And just then, through it came a gust
In a gentle swirl of silver dust
The curtains within seemed to fly
In the gust they rose, billowing high!

"It reflects this room so perfectly!"
"Look inside, see how you can see"
You, me, Sal, Mira and the coon
Mom, Dad, Leo and the magical moon!

But inside was more! A man, baroque
In what looked like a milky cloak
Like a toga, with a strange top hat
Rode the curtains like an acrobat

Flabbergasted, we looked on
At the bright, mysterious cabochon
From within he spoke "I will explain!"
It was the same voice once again!

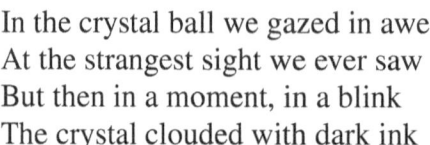

In the crystal ball we gazed in awe
At the strangest sight we ever saw
But then in a moment, in a blink
The crystal clouded with dark ink

We heard a soft flip flop, flip flop
Like the hoof-steps of a mare, up top!
It was just the curtains, blown around
In the breeze, with a flip-flopping sound

Translucent, white like a crescent moon
Billowing up like a half-balloon
The window curtains paused mid-air
Flip-flopping like a graceful mare

And there we saw him, quite a clown
"Stand back, ye all, I'm coming down!"
Just like the man in the crystal ball
Though now he seemed about to fall

Slipping down the curtain slope
Like a trapeze artist on a rope
He wasn't, though, in much control
Not with so much of swing-and-roll

Still clinging to a corner fold
He was quite a sight, to behold
Quite suddenly, the crystal ball
Cleared, and within, he seemed to fall

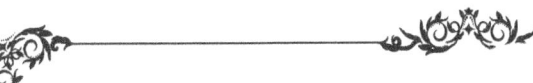

"I knew it! There's the silly toy"
"Stand back, will you? Down there! Ahoy!"
He jabbed at it, like a matador
And fell with a thud, to the floor

Look! Said Tommy, "Look! in there!"
In the ball was a comet, all a-flare
Whistling a song, like an Oriole
It landed "Plink!" in a crescent bowl

"I know it's here, the bouncing blot"
"I just know" he said, sounding taut
His voice grew soft, "I will explain!"
Then he said "I know!", once again!

Up then he sprang, like a spring
Like a pellet shot, from a sling
To the window sill he went, and splat!
He dropped the ball in his top hat

We stood still, mystified, perplexed
For everything just happened next
His hat turned, at the zephyr's croon
Into a bowl, like the crescent moon

A whistling sound came from afar
As a blazing comet, shooting star
Reached the bowl with a blinding glare
And "Plink!" it dropped in, with a flare

Then an eerie silence settled in
The flare grew paler, fainter, thin
With many sighs, the soft wind blew
Outside a barn owl sang "Too Woo!"

The magic book looked dark, solemn
Beside it lay the magic pen
The lines swayed fainter, up beyond
Like ripples on a silent pond

"Your star's gone!" With a startled cry
Said Mira, pointing to the sky
In the starry dancing troupe above
Were just a dozen stars left now!

"I knew, you see, I'd startle you"
"But I had to catch this bugaboo"
Said he, the rather portly soul
With a comet in a crescent bowl

He stood silhouetted in the night
By the window, in the soft moonlight
In his muslin toga, milky white
And sandals on his feet, wrapped tight

His hair was white, a scanty mop
Round a bald spot, like a turtle's top
His face was long, and even while
He was grim, it had a knowing smile

"Well, he said, but tonight, firstly
"Please accept my apology!
Since I knew of your first query
I knew this is where it would be

He said, referring to the ball
That magical harvest night of fall
"This crystal ball is not, you see"
"Just your average, ordinary"

With a lucky star in its hold
Its greatest powers could unfold
Good or bad, they could multiply
It could grow wings, and it could fly

Then Tommy, always so polite
Asked in a tone, still quite contrite
"We're sad we lost our question, Sir!"
"Will the magical moon still occur?

"Oh yes it will! I know that you"
"Will also have your question two"
"But Sir, how.." Leo blurted out
Do you know what's to come about?

We nodded, bobble-heads on spring
Yes, how did he know everything?
"Oh that!" He said, "It will make sense"
Still speaking in the future tense

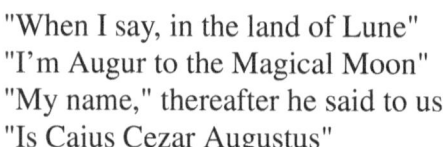

"When I say, in the land of Lune"
"I'm Augur to the Magical Moon"
"My name," thereafter he said to us
"Is Caius Cezar Augustus"

It was rather lengthy, as it was
But he continued, after a pause
"Vinicius Lipski Rabblerouse"
To a total silence in the house

"I had just composed a simple toy"
"As a gift to my messenger boy"
"A weather ball, that had a chime"
"To warn him just ahead of time"

"As I blew on it the final spell"
"I heard a "Go away!" "Scoundrel!"
It startled me, and then I, well
Forgot my runes, mis-spoke my spell

At that mistake, this baubled lens
Showed me a chase, and cakes and hens
Bounced and dodgded, rolled and veered
Sneered at me, and disappeared

But I knew I would find it here
That, at least was very clear
I knew because I would be tasked
To deal with a question wrongly asked

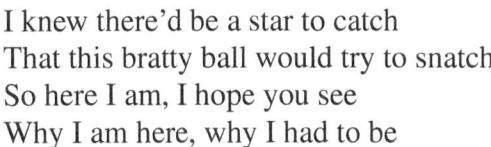

I knew there'd be a star to catch
That this bratty ball would try to snatch
So here I am, I hope you see
Why I am here, why I had to be

"Sir! said Leonardo, thoughtfully
If you can (really) always see
What lies ahead of you in time
Why were you startled at that time?

Ha Ha! He laughed, "there are, well"
Two things that even I can't tell
We waited, thought he'd continue
But his bowl took wings and off it flew

At this juncture, Mr. Rabblerouse
Expressively expressed his grouse
At crescent bowls and crystal flakes
At spells that had spelling mistakes

The curtains fluttered yet again
A moonbeam drove in like a train
Quick, Follow me! he yelled "Alight"
We followed him, just out of fright!

As we stepped in, we heard a din
"Disembark!" yelled Caius Kingpin
We followed him as he tumbled, smug
Right back on to our attic rug!

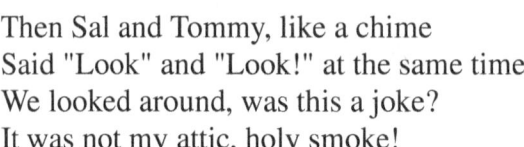

Then Sal and Tommy, like a chime
Said "Look" and "Look!" at the same time
We looked around, was this a joke?
It was not my attic, holy smoke!

Was a dark room with a fireplace
With drapes that were maybe made of lace
Strange shapes silhouetted, all around
From the ceiling to the ground

And then it seemed, some moving shapes
Appeared and drew open the drapes
A man stood there, dark with suntan
Said "Cezar! Hey, how are you man!"

We were in a room, fuschia pink
With things it was filled, to the brink
Arranged on tables, stools and shelves
Were trinkets, books and dolls of elves

Crystal balls with curious scenes
Like palaces with kings and queens
Cottages, cars and streets with snow
Dusky scenes with lights aglow

Mountains, meadows, rivers, plains
Thunderstoms and lashing rains
Homes and shops and village roads
Garden ponds with frogs and toads

And there was, on the mantelpiece
The crescent bowl! looking at peace!
Beside it, was a black top hat
And a crystal ball on top of that

By the fireplace, was a poker faced
Tall, slender man in flaming haste
T'was he who had exclaimed "Cezar!"
He'd been near us, but was now far

"And we have guests! How very nice!"
"How lovely!" Said an up-close voice
"Meet my good friend, Chris Crause, the great"
Said Caius, then he yelled "Wait, Wait!"

For Chris Crause was no longer there
"He's in his garden, out somewhere!"
But he blew back faster than a squall
Whereupon Caius introduced us all

Leonardo nudged me, whispered low
Did you notice that? How does he know?
Do you mean our names...? I drew close
He's an augur so.. maybe he knows

His "Hello..." was a little weird
For he instantly disappeared
His voice then trailed in "Very nice.."
From the garden of roses outside

For an instant there he pruned a leaf
"..to meet you!" he was back! good grief!
I drew a breath in to respond
But then I saw him by the pond

Where he arranged a border stone
While we stood in the room, alone
"Please" (he was back again) he said
Then "make yourself.." from the garden bed

"Comfortable!" . . . he now stood close
Then stood outside, pruning a rose
Then back again, with a welcome grin
By this time my head began to spin

"Thank you, though we do have to go!"
The Augur seemed unfazed in the flow
"That crystal there by your fireside. . . "
"What crystal?" floated from outside

Then zip!, he was by the mantelpiece
Exclaiming "Oh don't tell me, please"
"Oh where on moon did this come from?"
"Wish I knew.." he said, sounding glum

Soon as he made the wistful wish
The crystal, with a swirl and swish
Cleared, showed him in his usual race
Stopping each time at the fireplace

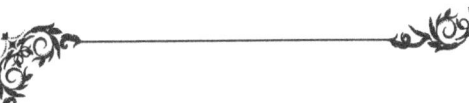

"On moon?" said Mira, eyes quite wide
"Caius! It's marvelous!" He cried
"How did you know? What a lovely way.."
"What a touching gift for my birthday!"

"Such a marvelous, marvelous thing"
He began to dance and then to sing
I can see now, yes, now I can see
What to do, oh this decides for me!

Then he flung his arms around Cezar
Thank you friend, to have come this far
Then Caius Cezar Augustus
Said, "Happy Birthday! From all of us!"

In the crystal now a clucking sound
Broke out, and in it, all around
Were chickens! Hens! A whole big brood!
Chris Crause instantly understood

"Oh dear, oh precious, oh what luck!"
Those must be Flimf Lam, and Snuck Shuck!"
Then the door flung open, what ensued
Was mix of hugs and a clucking brood

Warm wishes rang out to the sound
Of a brood of hens clucking around
A birthday farm, a chatter club
Filled with such clatter and hubbub

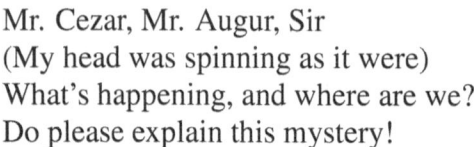

Mr. Cezar, Mr. Augur, Sir
(My head was spinning as it were)
What's happening, and where are we?
Do please explain this mystery!

Mr. Cezar lounged, like ourselves
On a velvet seat beside the shelves
His toga like pictures from Rome
In the rabble looked strangely at home

He began, "As Augur, I do see"
What time will bring, and what will be
But as I mentioned, there are, well
Two things that even I can't tell

The first one, here we now witness
A fine example, more or less
He looked towards Chris Crause, our host
Who was there one moment, then was lost

Mr. Caius Cezar shook his head
"How can I tell..," his voice like lead
"The future...," he said arms flung wide
For someone who just can't decide!

The second's why I had to chase
That cheeky crystal to this place
For no one should see, what or how
Will happen just moments from now

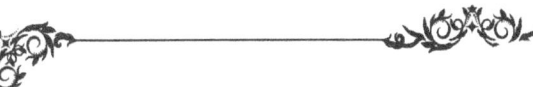

Its just not safe, he continued
You'd make mistakes or sudden moves
And such things aren't really fun
They are dangerous for everyone

Except for Chris! Who always runs
Does all of his work, all at once
He's talented, and very kind
But he just can't make up his mind!

For him this crsytal is a gift
Its really clear and very swift
He'd see in it, what he does next
And at least he'd never be perplexed

But I hadn't had a chance to tell
Exactly how my mis-spelled spell
Wouid unfold in what it brings
Contentment, joy or evil things

So I had to chase this ball around
Until it's true nature was found
Im glad it turned out well today
'Twas meant as a present, anyway

This is Fickleville, a town my dear
That's around the fields, very near
To the Magical Moon's grand fairway
It's where the most eccentric stay

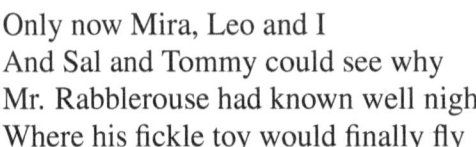

Only now Mira, Leo and I
And Sal and Tommy could see why
Mr. Rabblerouse had known well nigh
Where his fickle toy would finally fly

I forgot my spell, you your "why"
To Fickleville, so the ball did fly
As it would, when it ran amuck
It was also Chris Crause's good luck

Those are his cousins, then said he
Pointing to the trio, gazing in glee
Into the wondrous crystal ball
That held them very much in thrall

"We must go Chris!" said he to them
He was barely heard in the mayhem
We must go, he yelled, I have summons
Craus was again everywhere at once

He raced about, full time, full form
Like a blizzard, a nor'easter storm
Each time he stopped and took his cue
From the crystal, then he rushed anew

There's a party! said he from afar
Then up close, "Won't you stay, Cezar?"
"Next time!" said Caius, to Chris Craus
I know our paths will soon criss-cross

"All right!" said he, from the fireplace
Oh Flimf, our guests must leave this place
Would be wonderful, if you'd be
Around for this evening's fun party

And then I noticed, in a nook
A crystal showed a magic book
Through a window, and by it a coon
A starry sky, and a magical moon

A moonbeam came in, bright as day
"Goodbye my dears!" I heard him say
From the middle shelf, a railway guard
Blew a sharp whistle, loud and hard

"Disembark!" said an urgent voice
Whereupon we hardly had a choice
We ran behind him in a blink
There was no time to stop and think

Running fast from the room of elves
The next instant we found ourselves
Back in the attic, through the door
Like shells left pell-mell on a shore

There! said Plinski Rabblehouse
To a total silence in the house
Now I must really, really fly
But I know you have a final "Why"

I did! He'd almost read my mind
"Yes, thank you, Sir, you are so kind"
I asked my question, with a sigh
"Why did I, Sir, forget my why?"

And then he smiled the broadest smile
He'd known I'd ask this all the while
He said, "Its really simple so"
"Our future's enchanted, you know"

"If we knew what would be, how and when"
"We could not wonder or hope again!"
He vanished then, with a final twist
"Even magic then would not exist!"

The magical moon shone large up high
A million stars were in the sky
The crickets chirped and shadows flit
Outside the barn owl said "To Wit"

The pen doodled the faintest signs
Criss-crossing on the wavered lines
One moment south, one moment north
Vacillating back and forth

A leaf flew in, lay on the chair
There was still magic in the air
The clock ticked on, as if it knew
That it was time for question two

The Second Constellation

THE SKY on that October night
Replete with stars in the bright moonlight
Wasn't like the sky you knew
With the constellations you could view

It seemed a little rearranged
The constellations had been changed
The brightest stars within each pride
Had for this night, stepped aside

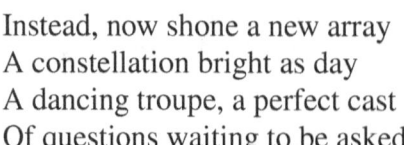

Instead, now shone a new array
A constellation bright as day
A dancing troupe, a perfect cast
Of questions waiting to be asked

Surely, a night sky's connoisseur
Would wonder who the dancers were
Just so they wouldn't be confused
I think they must be introduced

There was a star from Andromeda
One also from Cassiopeia
And one was picked from Lacerta
From Perseus came another star

An autumn star came from Cygnus
And there was one from Pegasus
Others trooped in from various
Homes like Aries and Cepheus

Some came in from across the sea
From celestia, which you couldn't see
From Phoenix and Aquarius
From the south, by Sagittarius

Then there was a mysterious one
From a constellation by the sun
Just far enough it was from your sight
That you couldn't see it on that night

It was named, on some royal premise
The great Corona Borealis
In the summer it had disappeared
But tonight its crown jewel appeared!

From constellations of great fame
Questions glittering in their name
Came to the troupe, caroused and shone
In a constellation of their own

The first one was called Sadalsuud
The luckiest star that ever would
Shine its light in the firmament
"Luckier than luck," the saying went

It was among the greatest ones
That could outshine a thousand suns
From the great Aquarius, known to some
As Lucida Fortunae Fortunarum

Like the flickering gleam of a candle wick
In its wake appeared Sadalmelik
Like a distant hawk, with royal wings
It flew in with the luck of kings

But as it neared it turned to be
Astounding in its majesty
Second in the row it stood
Brighter even than Sadalsuud!

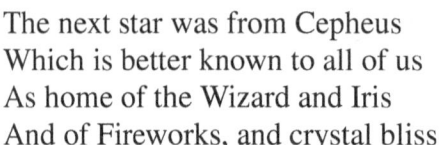

The next star was from Cepheus
Which is better known to all of us
As home of the Wizard and Iris
And of Fireworks, and crystal bliss

This third, a shepherd, called Alrai
Of the winds and seas, shone up high
Not much smaller and not too far
From the glowing crimson Garnet Star

Just as much a splendid cardinal
Was Andromeda's principal:
Mirach, its name a twisted word
With the power of a magic sword

The fifth star was from Pegasus
The brightest and most glorious
It was called Markab, and it was borne
By a swift enchanted unicorn

The sixth, from Cassiopeia
Was Caph, Al-Sanam or Al-Nakah
Lovely names for the very same star
On the palm of Cassiopeia

From Phoenix rose the seventh star
Of fabulous birds, this was the Czar
With wings like fire-wisteria
Flew in the beautiful Ankaa

The eighth was a mysterious star
From the constellation Lacerta
Its beacon bright, like that of fame
Though no one ever knew its name

From Corona Borealis one came
A jewel brighter than its name
This ninth star was called Alphecca
Or a king's jewel – the bright Gemma

The tenth one, of the golden fleece
From the constellation of Aries
Was a majestic star, called Hamal
With the golden-orange warmth of fall

The next one, also from Aries
Was Sheratan, of great caprice
It brought two symbols, each of which
If read, would to the other, switch

The dozenth one was from Cygnus
It was orange, large and luminous
This quintessential autumn star
For its wings, was called Gienah

The thirteenth star was an extremum
From constellation Triangulum
Made of magic, through and through
Of it powers just one person knew

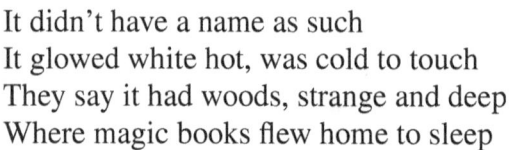

It didn't have a name as such
It glowed white hot, was cold to touch
They say it had woods, strange and deep
Where magic books flew home to sleep

A Goodbye

Goodby for now, my dear friends. The picture you see on this page is a glimpse of the actual view from my window. I see this often, lying in my bed at night, looking up from my pillow at the magical moon. Often, I feel weary and wistful, just wishing for more peace and more simplicity.

Life will go on. I hope yours is magical, and you can complete my stories in this book on your own.

On an autumn night, after harvest rain
The magical moon will shine again

Other books by the same author

A collection of whimsical tales, strange stories and funny accounts written in verse. Some excerpts:

The doctor, after he'd carefully read
My description, then asked, his voice like lead
If I'd knocked a wall against my head
*from **The strange disease***

This slimeball, in my living days
Was my lawyer, Howard S. Crook
"Surreptitious" was his middle name
Did everything by the book
*from **The haunting***

"A discounted tour!" it said multiple times
"Ninety-nine percent off!" proclaimed the lines
In so many ways did they display the sale
I wondered why it wasn't also in Braille
*from **A short trip to Japan***

A collection of poems of a philosophical nature. Some contain dialogs with life and the cosmos, some touch upon the raw essence of human experience, marked by hopes, fears, and the pursuit of happiness, while others just capture some serene moments in life. Some excerpts:

For each moment to happen as was portent
Every creature must follow the scribe's intent
And then I wonder, who could have divined
A billion short stories, so intertwined
*from **A billion sort stories***

An old library, it had books lined on shelves
Stories of old times, of kings, gnomes and elves
In the dawn light they glowed, musty and old
Each faded and bound, held time in their fold
*from **Dust***

In the coolness and shade, bare stones lay exposed
Stacked neatly in steps, led to doors that were closed
Doors carved of wood, thick and musty with age
For the stories beyond, each an opening page
*from **The alley of doors***

www.ingramcontent.com/pod-product-compliance
Lightning Source LLC
Chambersburg PA
CBHW071506170626
46811CB00007B/2742